Thick as Thieves

Also by Susan K. Marlow

Andrea Carter and the Long Ride Home
Andrea Carter and the Dangerous Decision
Andrea Carter and the Family Secret
Andrea Carter and the San Francisco Smugglers
Andrea Carter and the Trouble with Treasure
Andrea Carter and the Price of Truth
Andi's Pony Trouble
Andi's Indian Summer
Andi's Scary School Days
Andi's Fair Surprise
Andi's Lonely Little Foal
Andi's Circle C Christmas
Badge of Honor
Tunnel of Gold
Canyon of Danger
River of Peril
Andrea Carter's Tales from the Circle C Ranch

CIRCLE C MILESTONES · 1

Thick as Thieves

AN ANDREA CARTER BOOK

Susan K. Marlow

Kregel
Publications

Thick as Thieves
© 2015 by Susan K. Marlow

Published by Kregel Publications, a division of Kregel, Inc.,
2450 Oak Industrial Dr. NE, Grand Rapids, MI 49505.

The persons and events portrayed in this work are the creations
of the author, and any resemblance to persons living or dead is
purely coincidental.

Scripture quotations are from the King James Version.

ISBN 978-0-8254-4367-1

Printed in the United States of America
15 16 17 18 19 / 5 4 3 2 1

Friendship

UNSELFISHLY GIVING SUPPORT AND
EXPRESSING COMPASSION TO ANOTHER

*Finally, be ye all of one mind, having compassion one of another,
love as brethren, be pitiful, be courteous.*

1 Peter 3:8

CHAPTER 1

San Joaquin Valley, California, Winter 1882

Mother says a proper young lady regards her feelings as a petticoat—she never lets it show. If that's true, then I might as well give up on ever becoming a proper young lady. I'd burst if I tried to keep everything inside when something unexpected happens.

Taffy's in trouble. I know it.

Andrea Carter didn't say those frightening words aloud, but she couldn't help thinking them. Each time her golden palomino shook her flaxen mane and let out a sharp whinny, Andi wanted to jump out of her skin. "You're not supposed to drop your foal for another two weeks," she reminded Taffy. "Don't get ahead of yourself." She tried to keep her voice steady, but an invisible hand squeezed her heart.

Taffy's response was a jerky switch of her tail. Her hind foot went up and aimed a kick at her belly. She laid her ears back and paced the stall, exactly like she'd done yesterday. And the day before. When she passed the feedbox, she nosed the grain then tossed her head and kept moving.

"Something's not right," Andi finally admitted. When she'd seen other mares birth their foals, it usually happened so fast she missed the show.

She expected a strong, healthy horse like Taffy to do the same, even if it *was* her first time.

Andi reached into her pocket and drew out a handful of sugar. "How about a treat, since you turned your nose up at your oats?"

Taffy paused in her pacing to sniff the lumps but moved away. The next moment, she pawed at the ground and went down.

"Taffy!" Andi fell to the straw beside her mare. She ran her hand along Taffy's swollen flank and tried to stay calm. Nobody else in the family seemed to think Taffy's restlessness the past few days was anything out of the ordinary, but Andi felt it deep in her gut. Something was wrong. "Hang on, girl," she pleaded. "I know it's early, but everything's going to be all right."

She shot to her feet. "As soon as I find Chad, that is."

Andi didn't want to leave her mare alone, but if Taffy was dropping her first foal before her time, she might need help. Nobody in the San Joaquin Valley knew horses better than Andi's big brother Chad. "He'll see you through this," she called over her shoulder and raced out of the barn.

Low, distant thunder rumbled over the Sierra foothills as Andi sped across the yard. She looked up. The full moon glowed from behind gathering clouds. *Not another storm!* A heavy rainfall would probably be followed later in the week by the typical winter ground fog—a thick, drizzly mess that made going anywhere outdoors a challenge.

Andi clattered up the back porch steps, dashed through the kitchen and dining room, and burst into the library of her family's sprawling, two-story ranch house. "Mother! Where's Chad? I need him *right now.*"

"Mother's not here," Melinda told her from a low table in front of a crackling fire. "She had a headache and went up to bed." She fiddled with bits of velvet, lace, and dark-blue taffeta then looked up. "You better not disturb her."

Andi had no intention of waking their mother. She tossed aside a thick, dark braid and took a deep breath to quiet her racing heart. It didn't help. "It's Taffy. She's—"

"Not *again*." Melinda rolled her eyes. She picked up a half-finished bonnet and sighed. "You've gone on about your horse morning, noon, and night for the past week."

Andi turned a withering look on her eighteen-year-old sister. "If *your* horse was foaling and acting strange, you'd be worried too."

"Maybe I would," Melinda threw back, "but I wouldn't race into the house every ten minutes to yell about it."

Andi opened her mouth to snap out a heated reply then paused. Arguing with Melinda was a waste of time. And time was something Andi didn't have right now. She wanted to get back to Taffy. "Where's Chad?"

Melinda frowned her impatience. "I declare, Andi! Didn't you listen to *anything* at supper tonight? Chad and Mitch went into town to attend the first-of-the-year Cattlemen's Association meeting. They won't be back until later."

Andi groaned. She had been too wrapped up fretting over Taffy to remember what she ate for supper, much less pay attention to a dull conversation about a cattlemen's meeting. The minute she had been excused from the table, she'd rushed out to the barn.

Rotten cattlemen's meeting. What good were big brothers if they weren't around? "Why did Chad and Mitch both have to go to the same dumb meeting?"

Melinda didn't answer.

"If you like, I'll come out and take a look at Taffy."

Andi glanced across the room. Her oldest brother sat behind a large oak desk, occupied with a pile of paperwork. Ever since Father had been killed in that terrible roundup accident eight years ago, Justin had quietly taken over as Andi's substitute father. He was especially good at helping her, but he was a lawyer, not a rancher. She didn't think he could solve Taffy's problem.

Still, with Chad and Mitch away, it was worth a try. "Sure, Justin. But hurry."

Justin put down his pen and regarded her with a look that read *hold your horses.* "I have a few things to finish first. I'll come out when I can. I'm sure Taffy is fine."

"She's *not* fine," Andi insisted, leaning over the desk. "She's pacing and breathing hard, and not eating, and then she went down."

A slight frown creased Justin's forehead. "That sounds perfectly normal for a mare nearing her time. She's been restless off and on all week." He shuffled his papers. "Of course, if you don't want to wait for me you can always ask Sid or Diego to lend a hand. They're—"

"No!" Andi shook her head. No mere cowhand would go near her precious mare.

"All right, then," Justin said with a smile. "I guess I'm your stockman tonight."

With a sinking feeling, Andi realized this might be one of the last times Justin would be around to help her out of a scrape or give her immediate advice. He hadn't come right out and said it yet, but the whole family knew he planned to ask a certain Lucinda Hawkins to be his wife. *I should accept his help while I can still get it, before he marries Lucy and moves to town.*

She didn't want to think about that. "All right," she said, forcing her voice not to crack. "Just please come out to the barn as soon as you can."

"I promise," he said and picked up his pen.

Without a word to Melinda, Andi ran back to the foaling stall. Breathless, she unlatched the half door and swung it open. Her jaw dropped. Across the stall, her golden horse was standing and munching a mouthful of hay. She turned her head in greeting. *What's all the fuss about?* her dark, alert eyes seemed to be saying.

Andi stepped into the stall, speechless with surprise. A few minutes later Justin joined her. "It appears I rushed out here for nothing," he remarked with a chuckle. "Taffy looks fine, just like I figured. I think you'd better come inside and quit fretting over this mare. It's getting late."

Leave it to Taffy to make me look like a fool, Andi thought. But a finger of worry scratched at the back of her mind. "I want to stay out here a little longer."

"It's chilly and likely to get colder," Justin said. A rumble of thunder made him frown. "Sounds like a storm's coming up." He beckoned her to follow.

"Please, Justin?" Andi pleaded. "I'm all jumpy inside. The rain doesn't bother me. I want to keep an eye on Taffy."

Justin looked from Andi to Taffy then back at his sister. "Far be it from me to come between you and Taffy." He found two horse blankets and dropped them in the stall. "If you want to stay out here and shiver with cold, I suppose that's your affair."

Andi grinned. "Thanks, big brother." She might shiver, but she wasn't likely to freeze. The Circle C ranch lay in the valley near the foothills, not up in the snowy Sierras. She spread the blankets over the sweet-smelling straw and reached up to where a kerosene lantern hung from a large nail. With a flick of her wrist she turned down the flame.

"Keep a sharp eye on the lamp," Justin warned. "You don't want to burn down the barn."

"I'm always careful about that," Andi replied, stung. No one needed to remind her about the dangers of an unattended lantern. "It's safe up there."

Justin closed the stall door and leaned over it. "You're fretting over nothing, honey. Taffy's just restless. Let her get a good night's sleep."

Andi sat in the corner and didn't answer. Something was wrong. She didn't know what, but it ate at her stomach like a bitter medicine. Justin's cheerful words sailed right over her head.

"Chad and Mitch should be home before too long," Justin said. "When they put their horses away, you can ask Chad to take a look at Taffy. He'll tell you she's fine, then maybe you'll feel better and will go up to bed."

Andi nodded. "I hope that cattlemen's meeting ends soon."

"You and me both." Justin waved and disappeared into the shadows.

For the next few minutes, Andi watched her mare. "Thanks for making me look stupid," she said.

Taffy whickered. It sounded like a laugh.

Andi rose and brushed a light hand over her horse's back. An idea to pass the time popped into her mind. She reached past Taffy, into the space between the feedbox and the stall wall, and withdrew a felt-wrapped bundle. Returning to her spot on the blanket, Andi removed the covering and let a small, gold-gilded book and a pencil fall into her lap.

She sighed. If this were a dime novel, she would have read the whole thing by now. But it wasn't an adventure story. Actually, there was *no* story. The pages were blank. "It's customary for young ladies to record their thoughts in a journal," Melinda had said when she presented the book to Andi on Christmas Day.

Not this young lady, Andi silently retorted. All the same, she'd smiled and thanked her sister for the lovely gift.

"You should find a special place to keep it, so nobody"—Melinda had eyed their brothers with a teasing grin—"can peek at it."

That was easy. Stashed behind Taffy's feedbox, even Andi might forget where it was.

With nothing else to do right now, she picked up the pencil, cracked open her journal to the first page, and wrote: *January 2, 1882. I am sitting in the foaling stall with Taffy . . .*

Half an hour later, Andi slumped against the wall. She dropped the journal and pulled the blanket around her shoulders. Outside, the thunder grew louder. A flash of lightning lit up the stall. Rain splattered the barn roof. She yawned.

Andi was sure she was only resting her eyes when a high-pitched whinny jerked her awake. She sat up with a cry of alarm; her journal and pencil went flying. Overhead, the lamp glowed softly. Rain fell in a steady stream, but the thunder had passed on.

Andi sprang to her feet. She turned up the lamp and glanced at her mare. Taffy looked dark and slick with sweat. She pawed the ground, turned toward her tail, then whinnied again. A gush of water poured out from behind her. There was no doubt the foal was on its way this time.

Andi caught her breath. Shivers raced up and down her arms. *Taffy is having her foal!* Andi felt torn. She wanted to run for help like she'd done earlier, but if she left she might miss the birth.

When Taffy lay down and strained, the sense that something was wrong flooded Andi all over again. She saw the mare's muscles contract, but nothing happened. No little hoof peeked out. Taffy staggered to her feet and paced, as though trying to get away from the pain. Another contraction rippled across her flank. When it was over, her head drooped and she stood trembling. Her sides heaved.

And there was still no sign of a foal.

Taffy's in trouble, and I don't know what to do. But she knew who did. She snatched the lantern and prayed with all her heart that her brothers had come home.

CHAPTER 2

*I love Chad, but we have our ups and downs.
He bosses me; I aggravate him. I reckon
we're too much alike to really get along.
But there's nobody else I'd trust more to
help me with Taffy.*

Andi quickly made her way from the foaling stall at the back of the barn toward the entrance. She passed the stalls and noticed Chad's horse, Sky, and Mitch's horse, Chase, standing quietly. Ears pricked forward, they watched Andi with curious eyes.

She didn't stop to wonder why she hadn't heard her brothers come in. The beating rain drowned everything else out. They wouldn't have seen her lamplight clear in the back either. Andi fled the barn and broke into a run, holding the light high to find her way through the dark, rainy night. When she entered the kitchen, she heard the grandfather clock strike once from the hallway. One o'clock in the morning!

Did no one realize I never came inside?

She clattered up the back steps from the kitchen to the second floor. Her feet thumped down the hallway, the noise muffled only slightly by the thick carpet. She turned the knob to her brother's room and slipped inside.

"Chad?" she whispered. A shapeless form lay sprawled under the bed-covers. Setting the lantern down on the floor, she approached his bed on tiptoe. "Chad, wake up."

There was no answer.

All Andi could see was her brother's mop of thick, black hair peeking out from beneath the covers. She shook what she hoped was his shoulder. "Please, Chad. Wake up."

"Go 'way," Chad muttered. He rolled onto his side and drew the covers over his head.

Andi shook him again, harder. "You've got to come out to the barn."

Chad pulled the blanket from his head and opened one eye. "It's the middle of the night." He burrowed deeper under the coverings. "Go back to bed."

"No," Andi replied, near tears. She stood shivering with cold and fear. Her beloved horse lay in the barn, suffering—perhaps even dying. Taffy's foal might be in danger too. "You've got to take a look at Taffy. She's foaling and—"

"Good for her," Chad mumbled. "Let her . . ." A snore told Andi he had fallen back to sleep.

Andi took a deep breath. Her brother might react poorly to what she was about to do, but she had no choice. Not if she wanted to save Taffy. She reached out, took Chad's pillow, and gave it a yank. The pillow came readily into her arms. She stumbled backward and fell to the floor with a loud *thud*.

Chad groaned and sat up, fully awake at last. He gave Andi a dangerous look. "What time is it?"

"One o'clock," Andi whispered. She slowly rose and gripped the pillow to steady herself for Chad's reaction. Likely he'd yell at her and wake the whole house. Everybody would come running, and Andi would have to explain why she was awake at such an hour. *There's no time to explain*, she told herself. *Taffy needs Chad right now!*

Chad didn't yell. He just stared at her, bleary-eyed.

Andi blinked back stinging tears. "Please, Chad. You've got to check on Taffy. She's bad off."

Chad ran his fingers through his tousled hair and yawned. "I've been asleep for an hour." He squinted at her. "You're covered with hay. Have you been in the barn all this time?"

Andi nodded. "I didn't mean to stay out, but I fell asleep. When I woke up . . . oh, never mind! Just come with me."

Chad waved her words away. "All right, all right. Give me a minute to get dressed." He fixed Andi with a look that made her gulp. "If this is a false alarm, little sister, you're going to be *very* sorry."

Her brother's words rang in Andi's ears as she left his room and bolted out to the barn. She paced back and forth, clenching her fists each time Taffy unsuccessfully strained to birth her foal.

Chad's quiet catch of breath a few minutes later brought Andi around. She saw the sudden, alert look in his eyes and the furrowing of his brow as he entered the stall. "Taffy should have dropped that foal by now." He ran his hands down the mare's quivering flank and spoke softly to her.

"You can pull her through, right?"

"I don't know yet, but I'll do everything I can." He turned and looked at her. "You have to help me."

"I will. Just tell me what to do." Andi felt stronger now. Chad was here. If anybody could save Taffy, he could. He *must!* Wasn't Taffy practically his horse too? He'd—

"I need soap and water." Chad's sharp, no-nonsense orders jerked Andi from her thoughts. "Never mind if it's hot. Just bring me a bucket of water from the pump and some soap."

Andi lit a second lantern and hurried to do her brother's bidding. "Please, God," she prayed on the run, "show Chad what to do."

The night had turned pitch black. Rain splattered on Andi's bare head and ran in rivulets down the back of her neck. She found a bucket near the water trough and pumped the handle for all she was worth. Icy water gushed from the spout. When the pail was full, she picked it up and grabbed the lantern with her free hand.

Hurry, hurry! She tried to run, but the full bucket slowed her to a limp. Water sloshed over the lip and splashed her skirt. The freezing liquid soaked through to her stockings and dribbled down into her high-topped shoes.

Andi shivered. By the time this night was over, she'd be soaked from head to toe. "If only Mother would let me wear my old, *warm* overalls." Sadly, those days were over. A split skirt for riding was the closest she'd ever get to britches again. Unless, of course, she ran off and lived by herself in the hills like the backwoods, no-account Hollister clan.

Andi was not *that* desperate to escape growing up.

"Here," she gasped, setting the pail down next to Chad. Then she reached for the lye soap on an overhead shelf. She tossed the large, brown chunk into the water and waited for more instructions.

Taffy lifted her head and looked at Andi. She laid it down and whinnied when a ripple coursed through her body.

Andi choked back a sob. "*Do* something, Chad. I don't want to lose her."

"Take it easy," came his quiet warning. "There's no sense getting upset before we know what's wrong."

Chad was often impulsive and quick-tempered, but when it came to an emergency, he could be as patient and unruffled as Justin. He calmly dipped his hands in the icy water and scrubbed with soap clear to his elbows. He washed as if he had all the time in the world.

Andi shivered watching all that freezing water drench Chad's arms, but her brother didn't bat an eyelash. *Hurry up!* She clamped her jaw tight to keep her impatient words inside.

Trust him, a still, small voice echoed in her head. *Trust* Me.

Andi wanted to trust that God and Chad knew what they were doing, but it was much easier to believe it on a warm summer's day than in the middle of a dark and rainy night.

"All right." Chad shook his dripping hands in the air. "Let's find out what's going on. If you can get Taffy to stand up, it would make it easier on both of us, but she might not want to. Can you do it?"

Andi nodded. *Of course Taffy will stand if I ask her*, she thought. Why wouldn't she? Andi and Chad had trained Taffy since she was a foal. Surely the mare could trust the two of them to do what was best for her.

With soft words and a gentle-but-firm tug on her halter, Andi coaxed Taffy to stand. She tried not to cry out at how weary her horse looked. Taffy hung her head nearly to the ground; her whole body shuddered. It appeared the only thing keeping her on her feet was her loyalty to Andi.

"Good girl." She rubbed Taffy's nose. "Stand still and take it easy. It'll all be over soon. Chad's here. He'll make everything all right." Her words came out strong, but she trembled on the inside. What would Chad find when he examined Taffy?

Chad's sudden gasp made Andi's heart skip a beat. "Wh—" She clamped her jaw shut, not wanting to interrupt her brother's concentration.

"Uh-oh," he said a minute later. He sent Andi an astonished look.

"What is it?" She swallowed the lump that had lodged in her throat. "What's wrong?"

CHAPTER 3

There are some surprises I would be happy to live my whole life without.

Chad rinsed off his arms, straightened up, and held Andi's frightened gaze. "Taffy's carrying more than one foal."

"Twins?" Despair washed over Andi in huge waves. She'd seen twin foals once before—a long time ago. Both had been born dead a month before their time. Live twins were scarce as hens' teeth, one old cowhand quipped at the time.

This can't be happening, Andi thought wildly. *It's all a horrible nightmare. I want to wake up right now in my own warm bed, with Taffy safe in her stall and one healthy foal beside her. Not two. Oh, please, God, not two!*

Andi clamped down hard on her thoughts. This was no dream. She couldn't wish the twins away. She had to be strong and stay calm. She swallowed her horror. "Can you save them?"

When Chad didn't say anything, Andi knew he was getting ready to tell her a hard truth. He never lied to her, not even to spare her feelings. "I don't know," he finally said. "I'll do my best. Father and I saved twins once, years ago. And I remember another time when I at least saved the mare." He gave Andi an encouraging smile.

Andi didn't smile back. She was too scared.

Chad kept talking. "It's a bit of a tangle in there. Both foals are trying to make their way out at the same time."

"What will you do?"

"I'll try to untangle them and sort things out. Then I can push one back." He paused while Taffy unsuccessfully strained to push out a foal. "It's not going to be easy," he said, "and it has to be now. It's been too long already."

Chad took Andi by her shoulders. His hands felt like two chunks of ice, even through her jacket. "I'll do what I can," he promised. "But you need to understand something. We might lose the foals, and Taffy too."

Andi sucked in a breath but caught herself before she could yell "no!" She nodded numbly.

"Good girl," he said and dropped his hands to his sides. "You have to keep Taffy standing. Don't let her go down until I say so. It's important. Can you do that?"

Another numb nod. "Taffy trusts you, Chad. She trusts *me*. I'll tell her it's the only way. She'll stay up if I ask her to."

"Right." Chad plunged his hands into the bucket for a second wash. This time he shivered as he scrubbed. When he closed his eyes, Andi knew he was praying. It made her feel a little calmer, knowing Chad wasn't only counting on himself to pull Taffy through.

Strengthened by this knowledge, Andi worked hard to keep her end of the agreement. She talked to Taffy and stroked her nose—anything to keep the mare's attention away from what Chad was doing. It appeared as though Taffy realized her friends were trying to help. She never moved.

"I've got one of the foals lined up," Chad announced at last in a drained voice. "Taffy can lie down now."

Andi let go of Taffy's halter, and the mare immediately went down. She was fading fast.

"Please, Taffy," Andi encouraged, "you can do it." She stroked Taffy's nose. It lay flat against the straw-covered ground.

"Come here," Chad said from where he was kneeling in the straw. "Things should move pretty fast now."

Andi rose and stumbled to her brother's side. She was shaking all over.

With a quiet laugh, he reached out, pulled her close, and gave her a gentle squeeze. "Calm down, little sister. You'd think *you* were having the foals instead of Taffy."

Andi didn't laugh at Chad's attempt to lighten the mood. She fixed her gaze on the huge golden body in front of her and prayed silently. Surely God knew how much she loved Taffy!

A ripple passed over the mare's body. A hoof appeared. Then another. Right behind the long legs, a dark nose pushed out.

A tired smile replaced the look of worry on Chad's face. "I think we did it." He reached out to help deliver the foal. Two pushes later, a chocolate-colored foal lay quietly on the ground. Chad quickly ripped away the tough sack that enclosed the newborn.

Andi's heart skipped when the foal shook its wobbly head. Happy tears made her blink. She grabbed a handful of straw and wordlessly helped Chad rub the foal all over.

Taffy raised her head and showed a brief interest in her baby, then she concentrated on delivering the second foal. Once the first foal was out of the way, the second had room to turn. He slid into the world without too much trouble and with only a little help from Chad.

By now, tears were streaming down Andi's face. She marveled at the sight—one chocolate foal and one cream colored. They were beautiful: two little colts. The second foal took longer to recover from his ordeal, and Chad hovered over him for some time.

His next words brought Andi back to the here and now. "See if there's any hot water left on the cook stove. A warm bran mash might perk Taffy up. She's been through a lot."

Andi picked up the lantern and dodged raindrops back to the house. There was just enough water in the warming tank on the stove to put together a nice mash for Taffy. Andi stirred in a little molasses and hurried back to the barn.

Taffy perked up at the concoction's smell and worked her way through a good portion of it. Not long afterward, the mare shook her head and struggled to get to her feet, breaking the lifeline between herself and her foals.

"Good girl, Taffy," Andi encouraged her. "You've got to get up for your babies. Come on, girl. All the way up."

Taffy made it to her feet and stood still for a moment. Then she shook her head again and seemed to come to herself. She turned around and approached the foals, sniffing them delicately. Then she began the time-consuming task of washing them down with her rough tongue.

Chad sighed and stood up. "She's showing interest in the foals. That's a good sign. It means she's on the mend."

Andi let out a long, shuddering breath. *Thank you, God!* Then she threw her arms around her brother. "Thank you, Chad. You were wonderful! Nobody could've done better. I don't know what I would have done if you weren't here." She smiled up at him through tear-blurred eyes.

Chad gave Andi a crooked grin and turned her around. "Take a look." The foals, heads wobbling, were trying to stand. The chocolate colt had his back legs up but then he fell over into the straw.

Chad whistled. "That's amazing, considering what they've been through. They're a couple of mighty fine, strong colts to get up so soon. What do you think? Should we stick around to see if they need help with their first meal?" He winked at her.

Andi laughed. Wild horses couldn't pull her away from the barn tonight, and Chad knew it. *I wonder what time it is.* It felt like hours had passed, but Andi knew it couldn't have been very long from the time Chad stepped into the barn until the first foal entered the world.

Yawning, Andi sat back against the wall and watched the new family become acquainted. Minutes ticked by while she waited for the foals to nurse. It seemed that just as one of the foals stood up, the other tried and crashed into him. Then they both went down.

Andi shook with cold. Now that the immediate crisis was over, she felt the frigid night creeping in through her damp clothes. Worry gnawed her stomach. The foals were so little, and it was so cold. Each needed a bellyful of warm milk. How long would Chad wait before helping them?

"Can't we help them nurse?" she finally burst out.

"I'd rather they did it on their own," Chad said. "As long as they're strong enough to stand, we'll let them keep trying. If they start to tire, then we'll lend a hand."

Andi reluctantly agreed. Chad had brought the foals this far; she could trust him to finish. She pulled her knees up under her skirt and wrapped her arms around her legs to stay warm. She tried to keep her mind off the cold by thinking up names for the colts. But it was hard to think at all when she was shivering so much.

"You better get up to bed," Chad told her twenty minutes later. "Mother will have my hide when she learns you've been out here most of the night in this weather. I'll stay and make sure they get their first meal."

"I'm staying," Andi replied between clenched teeth. "Maybe *you* should go inside before you fall asleep standing up."

Chad looked exhausted. He leaned against the far wall of the stall with his arms crossed over his chest. His shoulders sagged. "I'm not going to bed only to be awakened an hour from now for some new crisis." He smiled to take the sting from his words. "If you're dead set on staying out here, we'd better find you something warmer. No sense catching a chill."

Too late. Andi had already caught a chill. She was grateful when Chad wrapped her up in the woolen blanket she'd used earlier. "There, that should help." He slid down beside her and wrapped an arm around her shoulder. "Warmer?"

"A little." She leaned against him. It wasn't true, but it was the only thing she could say to keep from being sent indoors. She snuggled closer and watched the foals.

Andi's shivering slowly lessened, to be replaced with a feeling of overwhelming weariness. Her eyelids fluttered. *This won't do at all*, she told herself. *I can't fall asleep.*

A slight shake to her shoulder told Andi she had done just that. "What's the matter?" she asked, jerking awake.

"I think it's time we gave these fellas some help."

The chocolate foal, whom Andi had named Shasta, had managed to stay up longer than ten seconds. He took three wobbly steps and bumped into his mother. Immediately, his short, curly white tail jerked back and forth, but he was poking around in the wrong place.

Andi tossed her blanket aside and gently pulled Shasta out from between Taffy's front legs. She guided the colt toward the mare's full udder and watched in satisfaction when he grabbed hold of a teat and started to nurse.

Chad brought the smaller colt, Sunny, to Taffy's other side. "This one's not as strong. He's worn himself out trying to stand and walk. I'd better make sure he gets a full belly before too long."

With a practiced hand, Chad put the cream-colored colt within a nose's reach of the warm milk. It didn't take long for Sunny to catch on, but Chad had to hold him up until he could get all he needed.

When Shasta had enough, he flopped down in the hay next to Andi. She stroked the foal and talked to him. Soon, Sunny also lay beside her. Taffy lowered her head and nibbled at Andi's hair.

Thanks for helping with my babies, she seemed to be saying.

"You're welcome," Andi said, reaching up to pat Taffy's neck. "But don't forget to thank Chad."

Taffy's head went up, and her ears pricked forward. She nickered softly.

Chad gave Taffy a friendly slap on the neck. "It was my pleasure." He turned to Andi. "Taffy can handle things from here. It's time to go inside."

"Go *inside*?" Andi clutched the blanket and wriggled down in the soft straw between Shasta and Sunny. She shook her head. "I'm going to wait right here while you run in and wake everybody up with the good news. *Twins*, Chad!" Her heart fluttered with the wonder of it all. "This is a world-shattering event!"

Chad chuckled. "Well, perhaps not *that* far-reaching. But it's rare, and Taffy's accomplishment will cause a stir around these parts. However . . ." He paused. "I'm not waking anybody up. There'll be plenty of opportunities to *ooh* and *aah* over the twins in the morning."

Andi gave in quickly. Her eyelids drooped. "All right, but I'm staying out here." She yawned. "I'm too tired to walk back to the house, and I'll be warm and cozy with the foals."

For an instant, Chad looked like he might try to force the issue. Then he let out a long, slow breath and nodded. "Suit yourself. You've earned it. But I'm going to bed. I'm done in." He picked up the lantern and turned for a final word. "You did a good job tonight, Andi. Mitch couldn't have done better. Father would have been proud of you . . . and so am I."

A warm glow engulfed Andi at Chad's words, but she was too tired to mumble more than a quick "good night" before her eyes closed and she fell into a deep, dreamless sleep.

CHAPTER 4

*Just when I'm ready to soar above the clouds
for joy, and everything's right with the world,
something sends me crashing back down to earth
and to everyday life.*

"Good morning, sweetheart."

Andi woke with a start at her mother's voice. Her eyes flew open, and she glanced around the dimly lit stall. *Are Taffy and the foals all right?* When she saw the cream-colored foal nursing, she let out a sigh of relief. Shasta, the other colt, lay in a corner watching her with quiet interest.

Andi rose from the warm hollow that had served as her bed. "Oh, Mother! Did you ever see such a lovely sight? Chad saved them all." She stretched, yawned, and looked around. "Where is he?"

Elizabeth Carter opened the half door and stepped into the spacious stall. "Chad has a ranch to run. It's late—nearly noon. He told me you had quite a night and needed the sleep." She smiled. "He also shooed away the gawking cowhands. But be warned, Andrea. They won't stay away for long. The ranch is buzzing with the news. Twin foals are a rare event, and everybody's eager to see them."

Andi nodded and shook the hay from her clothes. She couldn't wait to show off Taffy's new foals. If her friend Cory Blake were here, he'd propose she turn the twins into a money-making scheme. *"A peep show, Andi. At a dime a peek, you could get rich in no time."*

Andi muffled the laughter that bubbled up at the image: two dozen ranch hands paying to see the twins. And Cory would want his commission for suggesting it in the first place.

Elizabeth shook her head. "It's a wonder you didn't freeze to death out here."

"I was pretty cold at first," Andi admitted, "but Chad helped me warm up." She sighed. "It's over now and Taffy's fine. If the hands are quiet, they can peek in later, one or two at a time. I'll be right here all day. I plan to spend all my free time with—"

"The winter term begins next Monday."

Andi groaned. School. What a terrible word! Surely Mother would let her trade a few weeks of history and grammar for good horsemanship. "You know I have to stay with Shasta and Sunny," she said. "I need to hold them and rub them, and teach them to trust me. You know how *utterly* important the first few days and weeks are."

"So is your education, Andrea."

Andi waved toward Taffy, who seemed content to munch hay and let Andi do all the talking. "But how often do we have *twins*? May I stay home this once? I have it all planned. Chad helped me write a list a couple of weeks ago so I wouldn't forget what to do. I'll teach them to stop when I say so and to learn I'm the boss. Next week I'll put their halters on for a few minutes each day. After that, I'll—"

Mother frowned, which was not a good sign. "We've been over this before. I have no intention of allowing you to miss school and fall behind in your lessons."

"Why not? Half the class will disappear come spring, when the farm kids leave for planting time. Cory is graduating from the eighth grade this year. *He* doesn't have to go back. Why can't I graduate too? I don't care about school—"

"I do."

Andi slumped back on the straw. Graduating from the eighth grade was an important milestone for most of the scholars in the Fresno grammar school, but it meant very little to Andi. Mother was clear: each member of the Carter family would receive a full measure of education until they reached the "magic" age of sixteen. *Two and a half more years until I can be finished with this whole, sorry school business.*

Andi laid a hand on Shasta's white, fuzzy mane. It contrasted vividly with his chocolaty coat. He looked at her with dark, limpid eyes. *How can I leave him?* Andi looked at the nursing Sunny just across the stall. How could she leave either of them?

Her brother's words from nearly a year ago stabbed her memory. "You oughta wait a few more months before letting Sebastian visit Taffy," Chad had advised. "You'll have time on your hands come summer. Besides, who wants a winter foal?"

Andi didn't want to wait. The time had seemed right, and Chad didn't insist. Sebastian was a champion stallion and the perfect match for Taffy. Chad had shrugged and given his consent.

Now she was stuck with the results of her hurry-up attitude.

"You cannot say Chad didn't warn you."

Andi winced. *Is Mother a mind reader?* Then a new thought struck her. She listened. The rain had stopped. "Has the fog settled in?" she asked hopefully.

"No, but I'm sure it will eventually."

Andi rushed on. "It's nearly impossible to find our way to town when it's foggy."

The winter fog was often so thick Andi couldn't see the barn from the back porch. The thought of swimming through the icy, gray drizzle for an hour to get to town gave her a chill.

Mother's lip twitched. "You manage to find your way through the fog when you want to, Andrea."

Andi couldn't deny it. When the fog smothered the ranch for days on end, she rode Taffy high enough into the foothills to see the sun and feel its warmth. Just below, the fog hung over the valley in every direction as far as Andi could see. Still—

"Be grateful you have this week," Mother said, closing the subject. "You can get the foals off to a good start."

"Yes, ma'am." There was no point arguing further. Andi would have to make do with the one week of grace she had been given. It could be worse. The foals might have been born *next* week, and she would have missed a most enjoyable time with her new friends.

Surprisingly, the clouds stayed high, but the temperature remained cold. Andi led Taffy outdoors the next day. The twins scurried to keep up. Although her fingers felt ice-cold even inside her gloves and her toes were numb, Andi did not go inside except to eat or sleep. She wanted to sleep in the barn too.

Mother put her foot down. "Enough is enough. The foals will do quite nicely with Taffy at night."

One by one, each family member—and over two dozen ranch hands— took time out of their busy schedules to admire the twins and offer suggestions regarding their training. Andi's ears hummed with advice from well-meaning cowhands and wranglers. Old Sid, who had worked for the Circle C ranch for as long as anyone could remember, went so far as to examine both colts all over their faces.

"What are you doing?" Andi asked, puzzled.

"Lookin' for whorls," he explained. "Ya know, if they got 'em up near the forelock, they'll be difficult colts to train."

No, Andi didn't know that. When she asked Chad about it, he laughed. "The hands are a bunch of superstitious old 'wives' with their tales. Pay Sid and the others no mind. Cowlicks and whorls mean nothing, little sister. Good horsemanship means everything."

Andi was grateful for her brother's help. One afternoon she found a good use for the journal Melinda had given her. She copied the list she and Chad had compiled and added her own notes about training twin foals. Chad's advice was sound, and the colts responded as expected. At least Shasta did. Sunny seemed aloof and somewhat capricious.

"It's that whorl on his forehead." Sid smirked in satisfaction. Andi ignored him.

By the time school rolled around the following week, Andi had given Shasta and Sunny a good start. They understood "walk on" and "stop." They stood quietly most of the time and let Andi rub them all over. Outside they followed Andi around the paddock. Shasta, especially, seemed to prefer Andi's company over Taffy's. He galloped back to his mistress as soon as his belly was full.

The fog stayed away, and the winter sun turned warm by the end of the week. The only cloud on Andi's horizon came the day she had to bid her foals good-bye. With a long, disappointed sigh, she slumped in the buggy and headed out with Justin for the beginning of the winter school term.

CHAPTER 5

Training twin colts is a lot more work than I thought it would be.

The winter term of school dragged. Foggy or rainy days found Andi in the barn, brushing and handling the colts. She rose long before dawn to spend an hour or two with her charges before swallowing a quick breakfast and rushing out to the buggy. Most days, Justin shook his head and asked, "How many sentences will Mr. Foster assign you *today* for being tardy?"

Justin was not teasing, and Andi didn't smile. Her copybook was filling up.

Every day after school she made a beeline to the barn to work with Shasta and Sunny before somebody dragged her inside for supper. More than once, her brothers or sister found her asleep in a corner of the stall, nestled between the foals, with Taffy standing watch over all three.

"Please don't tell Mother," Andi begged Mitch the second time he shook her awake in one week.

"Your sleepy secret is safe with me," Mitch promised. Then he frowned. "Two active colts are twice the work. You need to pace yourself and get more rest, Sis, or you'll wear yourself out."

Andi refused to exchange her colts' training for rest. She cheered when the days began to lengthen. Wild poppies and a sheen of new grass in the hills helped sweeten her sour mood. The longer days gave her more time after school to teach the colts about creeks, flapping branches, and countless other scary things in the big, wide world.

It all came to a crashing halt one day near the end of the winter term.

"Andrea," Mother remarked at supper, "I ran across Mr. Foster in town this afternoon."

Andi didn't answer. Any kind of communication between her mother and the strict schoolmaster meant nothing good. The biscuit she was chewing turned to dust. She swallowed with difficulty and reached for her milk. At the same time, she frantically tried to recall if she'd been in trouble at school lately. Nothing came to mind. She relaxed.

"Don't you have anything to show me?" Mother probed patiently.

"I don't think so . . ." Andi's voice trailed away. She lowered her glass of milk and glanced around the table. Her family was looking at her with expectation. Luckily, it was *only* her family tonight. More often than not these days, Justin brought Lucy Hawkins home to share a meal. Sometimes he invited an important client from his law office to dine with them.

Andi preferred her school business not be aired in front of strangers.

"I don't know what you mean, Mother," she said. "I haven't been tardy for the past two weeks or in trouble for anything else." Mr. Foster had tapped her head the day before yesterday, but she wasn't asleep. Not really. He'd given her a warning, but Andi figured that didn't count as being in trouble.

Elizabeth shook her head. "It's nothing like that. Mr. Foster simply asked me what I thought of your marks." She paused. "He was surprised to learn I hadn't yet seen your monthly report."

Andi bowed her head. "Oh, *that*," she whispered in sudden understanding. She twisted the linen napkin lying in her lap. "I forgot to give it to you."

"You *forgot*?"

Andi's head snapped up. She met her mother's accusing gaze. "Honest! I've been so busy with the colts that it slipped my mind."

"Are your marks that bad?" Justin wanted to know.

"I . . . don't know," came Andi's hesitant response. "I haven't looked at them."

Chad laughed. "You must suspect the worst."

Andi's cheeks flamed. How right he was!

"Please bring me your report," Elizabeth said.

"Now? Can't it wait until after supper?"

Her mother sighed. "We won't put this off another minute, Andrea. I scarcely see you anymore, what with you hovering over your colts every waking moment. If you'd given me your report last week, we wouldn't be having this conversation now."

"Yes, ma'am." Andi shoved her chair back and rose without another word. Angry thoughts swirled inside her head as she hurried from the dining room. *Who cares about marks? I can read and write; I can cipher; and I know some geometry. I can spell, and my grammar is fair. What more does a rancher need to know?*

"I bet Chad and Mitch don't remember half of what they learned in school," Andi said when she was well out of her mother's hearing. "How often do they have to spell a useless word like 'pusillanimous' when it's easier to spell 'cowardly'?" The thought of her brothers conjugating verbs or mentally diagramming sentences while rounding up cattle made Andi giggle.

Her scowl returned when she entered her room. "All I want to do is help Chad run the ranch. I don't want to be a lawyer like Justin or 'finished' like Melinda. I got plenty of 'finishing' the two terms I spent at Miss Whitaker's last year. Now, where did I put that pesky report?"

Her monthly report lay exactly where she'd left it—tossed among a pile of odds and ends on top of her bureau. She spotted a worn copy of Mitch's latest dime novel and picked it up. The cover showed a lurid picture of a "wild Indian" crouched over a helpless settler, tomahawk raised to scalp him. She couldn't help thinking she was in much the same position—a hair's breadth away from being "scalped" over her poor performance in school the past month.

"There's no use putting it off," Andi decided, flinging Mitch's novel onto her bed for later reading. She took the yellow envelope and ripped it open. Pulling out a thin sheet of paper, she studied her grades for February. Except for arithmetic, all her marks were low. Grammar had slid to an alarming 71.

Andi bit her lip at the sorry truth of her inattention toward her lessons. *I'm in trouble.* She stuffed her report back in the envelope and left her room. For once, she didn't feel like sliding down the smooth, wooden banister rail. Instead, she plodded down the long staircase and into the dining room, where a lively conversation about cattle prices was taking place.

Without a word, Andi slid the envelope next to her mother's plate and dropped into her seat. Her food was cold, but she didn't care. Her appetite was gone. She waited while Mother pulled out the report and scanned it. The supper conversation had turned to teasing Melinda about her latest gentleman caller, but Andi had no heart to join in. She watched her mother's face for a reaction.

Elizabeth Carter's expression did not change. She folded the report and returned it to the envelope. "I see why you were in no hurry to show me this," she said. "It is quite possibly the worst showing of marks I've ever seen in this family." She glanced at Chad. "And I've seen my share of poor marks."

"Yes, ma'am," Andi said, eyes downcast.

"I needn't look far to find the reason," her mother continued. "The colts have taken every spare moment of your time, and your schoolwork has suffered because of it." She shook her head. "It's partly my fault. I should have realized twin colts were too much for you. I'm sorry I didn't recognize it sooner."

Andi's head snapped up. "They're *not* too much. Tell her, Chad. Tell her they're not too much."

"Don't lasso me into this," Chad said. "I've caught you asleep out in the barn more than once. A little time off might be a good idea."

Traitor! "Mitch?" she pleaded. "Tell Mother—"

"That will do, Andrea," Elizabeth said. Then her voice softened. "I think your time with the colts will be cut back considerably until your marks improve."

Andi paled at the thought. "By how much?"

"On school days, you will limit yourself to whatever chores you normally do for Taffy. On the weekends, you may have two hours in the afternoon."

"Two hours?" Andi couldn't believe it. The colts would forget everything she'd taught them. "What will I do the rest of the time?"

"Study."

Andi groaned. It was the worst punishment she could imagine. She looked at her mother in despair. There was no changing her mind, not once she'd made a decision. Not even Justin would be able to appeal on her behalf. Hot tears burned her eyes, but she blinked them back. She was too old to cry over such things.

"For how long?" she asked, keeping a tight rein on her feelings. She glanced at Chad, who gave her a sympathetic look.

"Until I see your marks back where they belong. Your March report had better show improvement."

Four weeks. Andi groaned.

"It'll go by real fast," Mitch offered cheerfully.

"Don't worry about the colts," Chad put in. "I'll see to them when I can. They won't forget your lessons."

Andi smiled halfheartedly. "Thanks."

"I bet your marks go up in less than a week," Justin added with a wink. "You're not one to drag your feet when you've got a good reason to do something."

Andi nodded. Justin was right. School might not be her favorite way to pass the time, but the work wasn't difficult. It wouldn't take long to turn those marks around.

For the second time that evening, Andi pushed back her chair and stood up.

"There's apple pie for dessert," Melinda said from the seat next to her. "Where are you going?"

Take a good guess, Andi thought. But she forced herself to smile and say, "If you'll excuse me, I'm not hungry anymore." Not even warm apple pie sounded good. "I reckon I'll go upstairs and start"—she paused dramatically and forced out the last word—*"studying."*

CHAPTER 6

*My schoolmaster says I daydream too much.
Maybe I do, but oh! It's so much more
interesting than history or grammar.*

*Record-breaking heat held the fairgrounds in its blistering grip. Andi stood
in the grandstand arena with Shasta and a dozen other weanlings and their
hopeful owners. From the corner of her eye she watched the perspiring, sober-
faced judge. He frowned and muttered to himself, just like the other two
judges had done a few minutes before. When he placed his hand on Shasta, the
chocolate palomino trembled but stayed quietly in place, head up, feet planted.*

*The judge moved on to the next colt—a striking black fellow who tossed his
head and shied away at the judge's touch. Andi tightened her hold on Shasta
to keep him from reacting to the unexpected movement. She turned a worried
look toward her family watching from the sidelines. A reassuring smile from
her mother and a grin from Mitch did nothing to soothe her nerves. Shasta
had to win a ribbon!*

*All too soon, the judge joined the others in a quiet huddle. Then he held up
his hands to quiet the onlookers. "We have come to a decision—"*

A painful jab between her shoulder blades wrenched Andi from her
daydreaming. The delightful vision of her beautiful, perfectly trained colt
winning first place at the California State Fair this August melted away
like ice in summer.

She sat up with a quiet gasp and found herself back in the stifling classroom of a late spring afternoon. Mr. Foster was regarding her with his usual impatient expression.

"Sir?" Andi swallowed and focused her gaze on the strict schoolmaster.

"I do not know where you have been, Miss Carter, but it is time to return to the classroom and concentrate on your lesson. Unless"—he frowned—"you intend to collect a number of failing grades on your next report."

Snickers rippled through the class of forty-plus pupils.

Andi flushed. She'd worked hard to bring her dismal, winter-term marks up to her mother's exacting standards, resulting in more freedom with her colts. But now the spring term threatened to once again plunge her grades down a deep, dark rabbit hole.

Andi flicked her gaze to the blackboard, where Cory Blake and Davy Cooper stood working. Davy was scribbling madly at a long-division problem, but Cory looked stumped.

A wagon box is 2 feet deep,
10 feet long, and 3 feet wide.
How many bushels of wheat will it hold?

Easy! Andi quickly worked the problem in her head. She loved arithmetic. A rancher fiddled with numbers, and not just to count cattle. Andi could figure bales of hay per acre or bushels of peaches per row faster than Chad or Mitch. She tagged along at livestock auctions to keep a running account in her head of what Chad bid on. "Saves me pencil and paper," he always said. Justin sometimes let Andi help him with the ranch accounts. That was great fun!

"Get your head out of the clouds and go work the problem on the board," Mr. Foster said.

More snickers.

"Yes, sir." Wiping the sweat from her forehead, Andi left her seat and headed up the aisle. These last weeks of school were proving the longest in the history of the world. Halfway through the month of May, a blast of unseasonably hot weather had descended on the valley, promising a scorching summer.

Worse, her best friend and seatmate, Rosa Garduño, had not returned to school for the spring term. Andi had pleaded, but Rosa for once stood firm. *"Basta ya!"* the Mexican girl told her. "I have had enough of learning. I had my *quinceañera* and am no longer a child." She had then given Andi a sly smile. "I am now marriageable age."

Nobody's marrying me off at fifteen, Andi thought with a shudder. Her big sister Kate had married at fifteen, but Andi had plenty of living to do before some fellow tried to lasso *her*. How glad she was that her brothers and Melinda were taking their time before getting "hitched," as the cowhands called it. After all, what was the big hurry?

Andi reached the blackboard and gave Cory a sympathetic look. Arithmetic and Cory did not suit each other. "As soon as I whip through my problem, I'll—" She broke off in dismay. The words on the blackboard were not an arithmetic story problem but a grammar sentence:

The stateliest building man can raise
is the ivy's food at last.

My worst subject! She glanced behind her shoulder at Mr. Foster.

He smiled. "You need practice parsing sentences, Miss Carter."

Andi felt drops of sweat trickle down the back of her neck. *I can find the subject and the verb, but . . . grammar failure, here I come!* She turned back to the sentence and closed her eyes. *I can do this. I just need—*

"Psst . . . Andi."

Andi opened her eyes. To her left, Cory mouthed, *Help me with my problem, and I'll help you with yours.* Cory loved words of all kinds. Grammar was like candy to him. She nodded eagerly.

Cory winked at her.

Andi flushed. Cory was a good friend, but winking was too bold, even for him. He'd never done it before. What was he thinking?

"I ain't goin' to school!" a voice hollered from the narrow staircase at the back of the classroom. "I ain't!"

Andi dropped her chalk and spun around, Cory's bold gesture forgotten. She heard scuffling, a loud clatter, more shrieking, and then a sharp slap. The next moment, a thin, straggly girl appeared at the top of the stairs. A rough hand propelled her farther into the classroom. She tripped and fell, then jumped up and clenched her fists. "I ain't goin', Ty!"

A large, scruffy-looking man with a dark beard and a slouch hat clomped behind the girl and grabbed her arm. "You're goin'."

The girl balked. She planted her bare feet against the wooden planks and tried to twist away from the man's grip. Clumps of tangled, dirty hair flew about her shoulders as she struggled. Her oversized overalls had been cut off; the ragged edges swept the floor. She lashed out with one foot, but the man was quick. He landed a sharp smack to the girl's cheek.

Then he turned and faced Mr. Foster. "Howdy, Teacher. Macy needs schoolin'. Mebbe you can learn her somethin' afore the term lets out."

Macy jerked loose and folded her arms across her chest. "This here's a hoity-toity school, and I ain't gonna be caught dead in it." She spat on the floor.

Ty, who Andi figured must be Macy's older brother, shook her. "Shame on you! What a way to act your first day of school. What'll these kids think of your upbringin'?"

"That I ain't got any." Macy looked around the room defiantly. "Look at y'all. A bunch of toads with your mouths hangin' open."

Andi, whose jaw had dropped at the spectacle, snapped her mouth shut. Next to her, Cory chuckled under his breath. "We're in for a show," he whispered. Andi agreed. This interruption was *much* better than dividing up a sentence into its parts of speech. To Cory's left, Davy Cooper put down his chalk and grinned.

Ty gave Macy another shake. "I'm gonna leave ya here, girl. If I find out you've run off, I'll take a strap to ya. Hear me?"

At this dire pronouncement, Macy lost her fight and become sullen. "I hear." She glared at the spellbound pupils. "What're y'all lookin' at?"

The entire class turned back to their work, except for the three students at the board. Andi watched with interest while Mr. Foster licked his lips and approached the strangers. "I am Mr. Foster, the schoolmaster. And you are . . ."

"Ty Walker. This here's my sister. We're new 'round these parts. Macy's wastin' time hangin' 'round the saloons and needs to—"

"Ain't true," Macy cut in. "You just don't—"

Ty clapped a hand over his sister's mouth and grimaced through his unkempt beard. "I'd best warn you. Macy's not strong on mindin' her manners. It comes from havin' no ma, but only a pack of scruffy brothers to keep company with. We ain't too good at raisin' no girl-child."

Macy peeled Ty's fingers away. "I ain't no *child!*"

Ty scowled. "Just do what you're told." He turned on his heel and clattered down the steps.

Macy's shoulders slumped when the door at the bottom of the stairs slammed shut. "You can't make me learn nothin'," she challenged the teacher from under filthy, too-long bangs.

"That remains to be seen," Mr. Foster said. "Come with me. I'll take down your name for the roll."

"Why bother? I ain't gonna be here long enough to—"

"Silence," Mr. Foster ordered.

Macy's cheeks turned red. She pressed her lips together and followed Mr. Foster to his desk. While the teacher opened his roll book and picked up his pen, Macy looked around. Her gaze fell on Andi and the two boys at the board. She stuck out her chin, crossed her arms, and tapped her bare foot on the floor. "Ain't you never seen a girl in overalls before?"

"Finish your problems," Mr. Foster instructed.

Davy and Cory whirled around, but Andi was too fascinated to turn her back on the scene. The schoolmaster gave his attention to the shabby girl in front of him. "Tell me your name, please."

"Ty told you. It's Macy."

Mr. Foster sighed. "Your *full* name, please."

Macy's foot kept up its nervous tapping. "Marcella Walker."

"And how old are you?"

"Jus' turned thirteen."

The pen scratched. "Where do you live, Miss Walker?"

Macy sneered. "I ain't no 'miss.'"

Mr. Foster looked out of his depth. "Please answer the question."

Macy blew at her bangs. "Me an' the boys live anywhere we want. We got us a place outta town"—she waved toward the window—"but it's a heap o' trouble goin' back and forth." She shrugged. "Most nights we find us a corner in the back of a saloon . . . or a storeroom . . . or mebbe sneak into the livery to bed down." She smirked. "That answer your question, Teacher?"

A thick silence fell over the classroom. Andi turned back to the board and pretended to work. She couldn't concentrate on grammar when visions of Macy sleeping in a saloon—or a drafty storeroom—filled her mind. It might work during warm weather, but what would Macy do come winter? What kind of brothers would let their little sister sleep in a saloon? *Chad barely let me stay out in the barn with Taffy.*

The silence deepened until Mr. Foster cleared his throat. He slammed the roll book shut and smiled wanly. "Well, Miss Walker, where shall we seat you?"

At Mr. Foster's question, Andi abandoned all thoughts of board work. The upstairs classroom was packed full this term. Although a dozen farmers' and ranchers' children had left during the last few weeks to help out at home, new students had quickly filled their seats. Fresno was growing into a lively town; it wouldn't be long before another grammar school would need to be built to hold all the pupils.

Her gaze turned to her double seat, where Rosa's recent departure left a glaring, empty spot. *Two* empty spots, since Andi stood at the blackboard. There was little chance Mr. Foster could miss it.

Andi scanned the room for another empty seat. *Any* empty seat. She found two more scattered among the girls. Another vacant seat was mixed in with the boys. That was all.

Her heart thudded. *Please, God, don't let Mr. Foster assign Macy to Rosa's seat!*

CHAPTER 7

I don't think Mr. Foster knows how to manage our classroom's newest pupil.

Andi stood, lost in thought, staring at the empty seats. A hand went up. "There's an empty seat next to Andi," Patricia Newton said. She smiled at her seatmate, Virginia Foster, and they both giggled.

Thanks a lot, Patricia! Andi wanted to holler, but she knew better. She glowered at the girl instead, which did nothing to keep her heart from hammering out of control. *Maybe Mr. Foster will switch some of us around. I'm a whole year older than Macy. She should sit with one of the younger girls, like Mary Beth—*

"Did you hear me, Miss Carter?"

Andi's stomach turned over. The piece of chalk she was clutching dropped from her hand. Her eyes focused on the schoolmaster. He had twisted around in his chair and was looking at her.

"No, sir, I didn't."

"You are excused from the board to return to your seat. Since I am sure you have no objection to sharing your desk with our new student, please take Miss Walker with you."

Mr. Foster's firm, gray gaze kept Andi from objecting. "Yes, sir." She heard Cory mutter "tough luck" when she brushed by him.

Macy was blocking the main aisle, but she stepped aside when Andi approached. "This way."

Macy grunted and followed Andi down the aisle. Her bare feet slapped against the smooth, wooden floor. As the new girl passed each desk, she brought her fist down with a loud *thud*, then laughed at the squeals and stunned looks.

Andi stopped next to her empty desk. "Here it is." She slipped into her seat just as Macy's hand whipped out. She grabbed one of Andi's long, dark braids and gave it a hard yank. Andi yelped her shock and fury. "Let go!"

Macy smirked and let go. Andi slid along the bench, scalp tingling.

"Hey!" Cory yelled from the blackboard. He ran up the aisle and wrenched Macy around. "Leave her alone."

Before Andi could blink or Mr. Foster could intervene, Macy threw a punch at Cory's face. Cory stumbled backward. His hand flew to his eye. Startled cries exploded from students all over the room.

Macy clenched both fists and held them up. "Just *try* to tell me what to do, boy." She jerked her chin toward Andi. "You sweet on her or somethin'?"

Cory stood his ground. His face turned red, and his left eye was already beginning to swell. Someone let out a low whistle. "That's gonna be a beauty," Jack Goodwin said from his seat behind Andi.

"Miss Walker, come up here."

Macy spun around. "Why should I?"

Mr. Foster rose from his desk, marched down the aisle, and pushed past Cory, who quickly fell into his seat. The schoolmaster dragged Macy to the front of the class and snatched up his ruler. Before she could react, the schoolmaster took her palm and administered five sharp raps with his ruler.

Macy's eyes grew wide and she giggled. "Why, Teacher, that ain't no more than a bee sting." Laughing, she returned to her desk and gave Andi a rough shove. "Scoot over. You're takin' up the whole seat."

"No, I'm not," Andi replied between clenched teeth.

Mr. Foster wrote furiously on the blackboard. When he finished, he slammed the chalk down and rounded on Macy. "Miss Walker, I do not allow disrespect in my classroom. You will copy this sentence one hundred times in your copybook. Then you—"

"Ain't got no copybook," Macy interrupted. "And I ain't been in no school long enough to learn what all the fancy scratchin's up there mean."

Mr. Foster gaped at Macy. So did the rest of the class.

Macy couldn't read.

"She needs to go back to Miss Hall's baby class," someone called. The class tittered.

"She needs a bath," Virginia whispered loudly enough to be heard.

Macy leaped up and went after Virginia. She took hold of the girl's pale hair and pulled. "You take that back, you stuck-up, simpering Miss Fine Airs," she shouted in her face, "or I'll snatch you bald-headed and—"

"Enough!" Mr. Foster peeled Macy's fingers away from his shrieking daughter's hair and sat his newest pupil down—hard—at her desk. Andi scooted clear to the edge, as far as she could go without spilling into the aisle. "Do not move from this seat until class is over," the teacher said. "If you do, I will thrash you soundly."

Macy glared at Mr. Foster, but the threat seemed to carry some weight. She threw herself back against the seat, folded her arms over her chest, and sulked.

Andi picked up her speller. She tried to ignore the dirty, ill-mannered girl sitting in Rosa's place, but it was next to impossible. Andi could close her eyes or look the other way, but she couldn't escape the stench.

For once Andi wished she carried a dainty, perfume-scented handkerchief like the kind Patricia and Virginia tucked into their sleeves. She'd never seen a reason for such frills before, but she saw their usefulness now. She could lift a hankie to her nose and disguise the odor coming from Macy.

How can I study with such a distraction? If Andi's grades fell, Mother would take away her privileges with the colts again. She looked to her left, through the open window of her second-story classroom. Springtime in Fresno was accompanied by clattering traffic on the now-dry streets, harnesses jingling, and whinnies and shouts. *I'm trapped next to this girl for a whole month.*

A sudden jab in her side made Andi wince. In a flash, Macy reached over and snatched the slate from Andi's desk. Too stunned to respond, she stared at Macy and rubbed her sore ribs.

"I need a slate," Macy hissed.

"There's one in your desk."

For an instant, Macy looked surprised. Then she raised a fist. "I reckon I got two now. Got a problem with that?"

You bet I do! Andi didn't say anything aloud. She turned back to her spelling book instead. Andi feared Macy's fist, but not so much as she feared being expelled from school if she took action against the rough girl beside her. Somehow she must find a way to put up with Macy's annoying habits without getting into trouble.

A real dilemma, and one not easily solved.

When Mr. Foster dismissed class, Andi was the first one down the stairs and out the large front doors. She took three gulps of fresh air to clear her nose.

"You better watch out, Andi," Jack teased, coming up beside her with a group of classmates. He plucked her sleeve and brought it close to his face, breathing deeply. "That new girl's stink could rub off on you." The others laughed.

Andi yanked her sleeve from his grasp. "You better watch out *yourself,* Jack Goodwin," she shot back. "Macy might give you a shiner to match Cory's."

Jack paled. Cory's eye was nearly swollen shut.

The others howled with laughter. Andi couldn't help grinning at Jack's sudden uneasiness. He was nearly fifteen years old. With the country boys working on farms and in the vineyards, Cory and Jack were the biggest boys left in school. Right now, though, Jack looked like a frightened little boy, all because of one bold and impudent girl.

As quickly as it came, Andi's grin faded. Macy stood barely a stone's throw from the cluster of chattering pupils. She could hear every word. In spite of her own disgust, Andi's stomach turned over in shame at her quick, thoughtless words.

"I'm glad *I* don't have to sit next to her," Virginia spoke up. "I'd swoon for sure." She patted her pale curls. "That girl is vicious. My head still hurts."

"And look at my eye," Cory added. "Does it look as bad as it feels?"

It did, but Andi slipped away before she found herself caught up with her friends in bad-mouthing Macy further. It solved nothing. It would only give the girl more reasons to hate her new classmates.

Andi plodded along toward Blake's livery stable, where Taffy waited. Not even the thought of being allowed to ride her horse to school while the colts were being weaned cheered her up this afternoon. *Shasta and Sunny must miss their mama terribly!* The colts were no doubt whinnying and carrying on in the paddock with the other young stock this very minute. Andi sighed. There was nothing she could do about it. The awful deed must be done.

"Why the long face, Miss Andi?" Sam Blake asked when she arrived at the livery. He led Taffy out of the dim building, bridled and saddled. "Are you still fussin' over those two young rascals you had to leave behind on the ranch?"

Everybody in the valley knew about the rare birth of Taffy's twins. She gave Mr. Blake a wan smile. "A little. But mostly . . ." She paused and drew a deep breath. "There's a new pupil at school."

"You don't say," Mr. Blake replied. "Seems no cause to let your spirits sag. What's one more scholar?"

Andi put her foot in the stirrup and swung into the saddle. "You'll see what kind of girl she is when Cory gets home."

"Will I now?" Mr. Blake scratched the back of his neck. "A new girl, eh? Is she pretty? Did Cory take a liking to her? Is that why you're droopy? A mite jealous, are ya?" he teased.

Andi's stomach flip-flopped. What was Mr. Blake driving at? *Cory's one of my best friends, but . . . does he think I like him* that *way?* She felt her face flame, just like it had when Cory winked at her at the blackboard. Did he think of her as more than his best fishing chum? *He better not!*

Andi squirmed in her saddle. She didn't want to think about that right now.

Mr. Blake grinned at Andi's fidgeting. "Did she give my Cory a kiss?" he asked, hands on his hips.

Andi choked back laughter, her spirits suddenly restored. "No indeed, sir. Nothing like that. Quite the opposite." She pulled Taffy around and waved good-bye to the friendly livery man. "But thanks for cheering me up!" She touched her mare lightly in the sides and headed for home.

CHAPTER 8

I'm in a terrible fix—and not one of my own making this time. I feel that if something doesn't change at school, I'm going to do something I'll regret.

"There's a new girl at school," Andi announced at supper that night. "She's the coarsest, most ill-mannered person I ever met. Worse, Mr. Foster assigned her Rosa's old seat. I can't sit by Macy. Could somebody talk to the schoolmaster for me?"

Nobody answered her. Andi sighed. She might as well be out in the barn talking to Taffy.

Melinda leaned over. "You won't get a word in edgewise tonight, Andi. Chad's all worked up over the missing cattle. You should've heard him hollering this afternoon." She rolled her eyes and went back to her plate of beef and potatoes.

Andi's heart jumped to her throat. Her trouble with Macy flew out of her head. "What missing cattle?" She frowned. As usual, all the interesting things happened when she was away at school. She nudged Melinda. "*What* missing cattle?" she repeated, louder this time.

Chad flicked an impatient glance in her direction. "Nothing you need to worry your head over." Without waiting for a response, he returned to the discussion he was carrying on with Justin and Mitch.

Andi flushed. Chad had brushed her away as if she were six years old.

Well, that old adage "children should be seen and not heard" did not apply to a young lady who would shortly be turning fourteen. "I'm part of this family too," she told him. "Why am I always the last one to learn about anything exciting?"

"Cattle rustling is not something to get excited about," Justin said. "It's a dangerous business—full of long, sleepless nights and stretched nerves." He glanced at Chad, whose nerves already looked stretched tighter than a cinched-up horse's belly.

"Not to mention the stretched necks when we catch the thieves," Mitch put in with a grin.

Nobody laughed at Mitch's attempt to lighten the mood.

"*If* we catch them," Chad muttered. He turned to Justin. "How many cattle did we lose last time? Two hundred head? Three hundred? By the time we figured out who was behind the operation, the gang of rustlers had hightailed it clear to Nevada." His face turned dark.

Andi suddenly wished she hadn't been so quick to ask about missing cattle. Rustling was her family's worst nightmare. She remembered four years ago when Carter beef had gone missing. The entire household remained in an uproar for nearly a month, until the crisis blew over. It had not ended well. Ever since, any mention of cattle rustling sent Chad on a rant.

He was ranting now in grim memory. "They got away scot-free with not only our beef, but with McClellan's and Jacobson's too. They've probably got themselves a nice little spread somewhere, a spread started with *our* cattle." Chad slammed his fist down, rattling the silver and startling Andi half out of her wits.

She swallowed, *very* sorry she'd pressed to be included in the conversation. Once Chad got started on a subject, he was nearly impossible to rein in until he'd had his full say. Instead of discussing the current crisis, he was now embroiled in the past.

Elizabeth took a sip of water and broke into Chad's tirade. "We would all appreciate it if you chose a place other than the supper table to vent your frustration," she said quietly. "Preferably out on the range, where only the livestock need put up with it."

"It would probably cause a stampede," Melinda whispered to Andi.

Andi giggled. Chad's temper was a well-worn joke. Melinda's comment quickly restored Andi's spirits. But not for long.

"You girls find this funny?" Chad slapped another slice of roast beef onto his plate. His blue eyes flashed with annoyance at what lay ahead for himself and his men over the next few weeks.

"Certainly not," Melinda replied primly. She lifted her napkin to her lips to hide her smile.

"No, Chad," Andi hastily added. "Cattle rustlers don't sound funny at all. I'm sorry I asked." She was even sorrier she'd tried to bring up the subject of Macy. There was little hope anyone would be interested in her petty school problems tonight. Not with the ranch in upheaval over real trouble.

It wasn't that Andi didn't care about the missing cattle. She did care. She lived on a cattle ranch. But honestly! A few missing *cows*? Now, if someone were stealing Circle C horses, that would be another matter. Her heart fluttered fearfully at the thought.

"I hope this new threat can be dealt with quickly," Mother said, "for all our sakes. What are your plans so far?"

Chad let out a deep breath before answering. At least he wasn't pounding the table any longer. "First of all," he said, "I don't care how much it costs or how many extra men I have to hire. I plan to nip this rustling operation in the bud."

Andi envisioned plenty of banging around and bossing over the next month. She planned to stay out from underfoot for however long it took her family to resolve this dilemma. One glance at Justin told her she'd better stay *far* away, even from her oldest and favorite brother. He didn't look pleased at the prospect of taking time off from his law practice to go after cattle rustlers.

I bet he won't be spending much time with Miss Lucinda Hawkins either,

Andi thought. *I wonder how she'll feel about that.* In times of crisis, the entire Carter clan pitched in. If Lucy hoped to become part of the family, it was best she learned this before the "I do" and not afterward.

Andi turned a deaf ear to the rest of Chad's plans and kept quiet. Her brothers would not appreciate what she was thinking. *Who cares about missing cows? Right now, I've got a much bigger problem than cattle rustlers.*

Andi's problem had a name—Macy Walker—and as yet she had no solution. She ate in silence while she tried to figure out what to do. If Macy continued to harass her, Andi would eventually react, even if she steeled herself not to. No matter how many Bible verses she memorized about loving your enemy or not returning evil for evil, Andi knew her own heart. She always struggled to keep her temper reined in, just like Chad.

"I'm going out to see the colts," Andi announced when she finished her meal. The hope of sharing her problem with a sympathetic ear at supper fizzled away. Chances were that every meal conversation for the next month would be taken up with rustler talk.

Mother nodded her permission, but nobody else even acknowledged she'd spoken.

"I think I'll join you," Melinda said, pushing back her chair. "Since I'm not a candidate for night duty, I'll keep myself busy elsewhere." She gave the boys a pointed look, which showed Andi that her sister was not any happier with the supper conversation than she was.

Andi was delighted that Melinda wanted to come along. The colts were great fun, but they were just a distraction this evening. Andi was desperate for advice, and Mother seemed preoccupied with the rustling. *Perhaps Melinda can help.*

The girls made their way to the grassy paddock beyond the horse barn, where two dozen young horses were grazing. A clump of valley oaks provided shade, and a wide irrigation ditch cut across the southeast corner of the large enclosure. It wasn't as fun as splashing in a real creek, but this pasture was one of Andi's favorite places to go—especially since her colts had graduated to it.

"Shasta! Sunny!" Andi hoisted herself up on the top railing. She lifted two fingers to her lips and gave a loud, clear whistle.

Her colts were not the only ones to answer the call. A big yearling paint horse raced to be first, leaving the younger horses in his wake. He pranced and frisked, then thrust his head into Andi's lap, nearly knocking her off the fence.

"Whoa there, Apache." She grabbed the fence post for support. "Simmer down." She shoved the paint's nose aside and jumped into the pasture. Shasta and Sunny jostled each other to claim Andi's attention. She shooed the other horses away. They snorted and headed for Melinda, who had entered the paddock through the gate.

"Hello, my little beauties." Andi stood between Shasta and Sunny, stroking their heads and scratching their itchy spots. They were no longer little. Andi was amazed when she remembered their tiny bodies and uncertain start in life almost five months ago. Now the colts were big, strapping animals full of health and high spirits.

Andi couldn't decide which foal was her favorite. Sunny, the smaller colt, looked like a sunbeam. He had a mischievous, impulsive air about him and startled unexpectedly. At times Chad had to intervene to keep him in line. He warned Andi to stay on top of his training.

"Then there's you, Shasta." Andi stroked the flaxen mane so like Taffy's. The resemblance to his dam ended there. His coat was dark chocolate, with no socks or stripes to break it up. Smart as a whip and calm as a summer's day, Shasta always managed to edge his way closest to Andi's side.

With the young horses following close at their heels, Andi and Melinda strolled around the pasture. By the time they reached the grove of oak trees, most of the herd had wandered off, leaving only the twins. They lingered near Andi as if she were their mother. No doubt they missed Taffy.

Weaning is never any fun, Andi thought. She plopped down in the shade of an oak and leaned back. Without meaning to, she sighed.

"Feeling sorry for your colts?" Melinda asked, smacking Sunny on the chest when he ventured too near. The colt backed off, shook his mane, and nipped Shasta. Shasta flattened his ears. "Or is it more serious, like you hinted at supper when nobody was listening?"

"It's serious. And I have to solve it before school tomorrow."

"Tell me about it," Melinda said. She lowered herself to the ground beside Andi and smiled. "See? I like sitting on the grass occasionally."

Andi wrinkled her forehead. *Melinda must really be feeling sorry for me.* "Aren't you afraid you'll get your dress wrinkled or grass stained? I thought Peter was coming by to take you for a buggy ride."

A twinge of satisfaction surged through her at the mention of Peter. Melinda's former beau, the shifty-eyed Jeffrey Sullivan, was now a specter of the past. He'd been exposed last summer for who he really was—a shallow, dishonest fellow.

Andi had jumped for joy when Peter Wilson asked permission to call on Melinda. He never talked about last fall, when he finally confessed he'd killed a man in a fair fight. Nor did he mention the dead man's daughter, Megan, who had packed up her little brother and left town soon after the trial.

Andi didn't pry. Peter had made things right and clearly wanted to get on with his life.

Melinda brushed a stray lock of golden hair from her face. "Peter's not coming until tomorrow evening. So, tell me. What was all that at supper about a new girl and having to sit with her? Is she really that bad? Maybe I can help."

Andi smiled. It was hard to imagine Melinda being able to help. She never found herself in the predicaments Andi stumbled into. But Andi needed advice, and Mother was not available. She took a deep breath and poured out her worries. For extra sympathy, she included a description of Macy's general appearance and unpleasant odor.

Melinda wrinkled her nose and listened without interrupting. When Andi ran out of steam, Melinda propped her chin in her hands and crinkled her forehead into what Andi recognized as her sister deep in thought.

Five minutes passed. Then ten. "Well?" Andi finally burst out. "What should I do?"

Melinda smoothed her skirt. "Why do you suppose Macy acts the way she does?"

"Huh?" Andi shrugged. "How should I know? She's just mean—*rattlesnake* mean."

"Did you ever stop to think about *why* she's mean? From what you told me, it sounds like nobody cares about this girl enough to see that she has clean clothes or takes a bath. Her scruffy brother sure doesn't sound like . . . well, like Justin, for instance."

"That's for sure." As far as Andi could tell, Ty Walker was the complete opposite of *any* of her brothers. A twinge of compassion for Macy tickled the back of her mind. Appreciation for her own brothers quickly followed. Chad gave up a good night's sleep to save Taffy and the colts last winter. She mentally let his brusque manner at supper slip away like water off a duck's back.

"She could be hiding a lot of hurts under that mean shell of hers," Melinda was saying. "She's probably ashamed of the way she looks and smells, or the fact that she can't read. Maybe she's been ridiculed in other places and made to feel worthless."

"Nobody would dare laugh at her for long," Andi said. "You should see what she did to Cory's eye." She tossed a handful of grass into the air and watched it flutter down on her skirt. "I don't want to go to school tomorrow."

Melinda laughed. "You *never* want to go." Then she turned serious. "School will be out in a month. My advice is to sit tight, mind your own business, and ignore Macy."

"Easy for you to say!" Andi snapped. Then she winced. "Sorry, I know you're only trying to help. But how do I ignore the stink? Or the poking? Or Macy stealing my things?"

Melinda shrugged. "All right then. Why don't you simply ask Mr. Foster for a new seat? Things might go smoother if Macy were left to herself and had no one to pester."

Andi gaped at her sister in astonishment. "What a splendid idea, Sis! It's so simple, I don't know why I didn't think of it. Thank you!"

The huge stone that had threatened to settle permanently in Andi's stomach dissolved into nothingness. She smothered Melinda in an enormous hug then jumped up and dashed across the field to romp with the colts.

CHAPTER 9

Mr. Foster is full of surprises . . . and he hits you with them when you least expect it.

With a faint hope that Macy's experience yesterday had soured her from further school attendance, Andi left Taffy at the livery early the next morning. She didn't wait for Cory to walk to school with her. His light-hearted chatter would not sit well with her mood. Besides, ever since Mr. Blake had teased her, she felt unsettled.

It didn't help when Rosa whispered to her late last night that Hector Flores, a young *vaquero* from the Bent Pine ranch, had asked her *papá* permission to come calling. When Andi's jaw dropped, Rosa had giggled and ducked her head.

Cory better not get any ideas beyond racing or fishing, she thought fiercely. *What a way to ruin a perfectly good friendship.*

Andi shook her head to banish such thoughts and picked up her pace. As she walked, she fingered the thin *McGuffey's* reader she'd slipped into her skirt pocket on a whim. It was her old primer—a child's first reader. She wondered if she was asking for trouble if she offered the book to Macy.

She'll probably throw it back in my face, she thought bleakly.

Andi didn't know why she'd spent an hour last night looking for the worn primer, or why she wanted to hand it over to the likes of Macy Walker. Did she need to prove to herself that she didn't dislike her as much as she'd let on to Melinda?

Andi shook her head. No, that wasn't it. A peace offering? Andi bit her lip and faced the cold, hard truth: Macy scared her. She was as unpredictable as a wild horse. Hadn't Cory experienced her hair-trigger temper?

"If Macy can do that to a big, strong boy like Cory, what might she do to me?" Andi was ashamed to admit it, but she hoped Mr. Foster would find enough fault with Macy to expel her from the classroom.

Andi scolded herself for her uncharitable thoughts while she crossed the deserted schoolyard. She quickly entered the building and stopped short. The place felt eerily quiet with no pupils running around and hollering. Feeling like an intruder, she tiptoed up the wooden steps toward her classroom. She clutched the little book tighter. "I'll give her the primer," Andi whispered, "but Mr. Foster better give me a new seat . . . *or else.*"

Or else what? Halfway up the stairs, Andi's confidence wavered. The solution Melinda had presented yesterday suddenly didn't seem like such a good idea now that she was only a few moments away from having to ask. Her hands felt sweaty.

Mr. Foster doesn't even like me. Ever since she'd run him down on his first day in Fresno, Andi and he had not agreed on anything. The schoolmaster had, however, softened a bit after Andi took his daughter Virginia's place as a hostage. He even praised her for her selfless decision.

"I doubt he'll praise me for *this* request," Andi mumbled as she neared the top of the stairs. "What I'm asking for isn't selfless at all."

Armed with the primer in one hand and as humble a spirit as she could manage in the other, Andi stepped into the silent classroom. The schoolmaster sat at his desk, grading what looked like yesterday's composition essays. Andi waited at the back of the room. Her heart thumped loudly in her ears.

A long minute later, Mr. Foster raised his head and gave Andi a curious look. His gaze flicked to the wall clock; the hands pointed at twenty to nine. "Is there something you need, Miss Carter? You're not usually the first to arrive."

Before she could change her mind, Andi shot up the aisle. Her shoes

clattered loudly against the wooden floor. "Please, Mr. Foster," she burst
out when she came to a stop in front of his desk. "Would you put me at
another desk? I know there are two or three empty ones. The seat next to
Mary Beth is not being used. May I sit with her?"

"Wha—"

"I'll take *any* seat." Andi's words poured out like a flood. "Even if it
means sitting with the boys. I'll sit in the back corner with Kevin or with
Ollie." She gulped. "I'll even sit on the dunce's stool. Anywhere but—"

"What on earth are you going on about?" Mr. Foster interrupted. His
expression had gone from mild curiosity to bewilderment.

Andi took a deep breath and kept talking. "I'll wear my Sunday best
to school the rest of the term, and I'll act like such a lady you'll never
recognize me. I really can act like a lady if I put my mind to it. Just please
don't make me sit with Macy. I'll crowd in anywhere else." She held her
breath and waited.

"Andrea!" Mr. Foster said, clearly astonished. "You look positively dis-
traught. I'm surprised. I've been under the impression these last two years
that you like challenges."

Andi shook her head. Misery filled her. "No, sir. Not this kind." Her
hands shook, so she dropped the primer into her pocket and clasped her
hands behind her back. "I can't sit by Macy. Will you please move me
to another seat?" *Please, God. Talk to him right now. Tell him to give me
another seat!*

Mr. Foster leaned back in his chair, crossed his arms, and looked at
her. He didn't say a word. Andi had a feeling he was savoring the moment.
Shame washed over her. She'd begged for a new seat, just like an anxious,
whiny child. She wished she had a note from her mother to slap down
on his desk. Or better yet, a note from Justin, who was a school-board
member, demanding that the schoolmaster change her seat. *Why didn't I
think of that?*

Finally, the schoolmaster spoke, and Andi's daydream went *poof.*
Neither Mother nor Justin would have agreed to write a note anyway.

"I wish I could accept your interesting offer," Mr. Foster said, smiling a little. "I am sure it would be a memorable experience for us all." He shook his head and lost his smile. "But I'm sorry. I can't do what you ask."

Andi sagged inwardly. *You're sorry?* To her surprise, her teacher really did sound sorry. "Is it because of the fall term two years ago?" she asked.

Mr. Foster gave her a blank look.

"You know. Your first term, when Taffy and I ran you down. You've never cared for me since."

The schoolmaster's dark-gray eyes opened wide. "I put that unpleasant incident behind me long ago, Andrea, as you should have also. I'm sorry you've interpreted my actions toward you as dislike. I don't dislike you at all."

"Then why did you stick Macy with *me* when there are other seats available?" Her words came out accusing, and she steeled herself for a reprimand. She was questioning the schoolmaster's authority, something Mr. Foster did not tolerate, and neither did the school board.

He leaned forward, folded his hands, and rested them on the stack of composition papers. Instead of a harsh scolding, his voice grew soft. "I put Marcella Walker with you, Miss Carter, because I believe that of all the girls in this classroom, you are the only one capable of coping with her."

Andi's stomach turned over. "Me?" *That's not true*, she wanted to argue, but Mr. Foster didn't give her a chance.

He held up a hand for silence. "Tell me then. With whom shall I seat her? Mary Beth Sharp? Abigail Turner? Your friends Rachel or Margaret?" He shook his head. "No, Macy will make life miserable for any of the girls in this classroom, and for most of the boys too, I fear."

"And she won't make *my* life miserable, sir?" Andi choked out. Anger and revulsion made her stomach churn. Why couldn't Macy sit by herself? Mr. Foster's stubborn refusal to move Andi proved he still held a grudge against—

"You won't let her."

Those four words doused Andi's fire faster than a bucket of cold water and left her dumbstruck. What did the schoolmaster mean?

Mr. Foster caught her look and sighed. "You Carters . . ." He shook his head, as if there was no understanding Andi's family. "You have a way about you that makes me think you can handle just about anything. You are not my idea of a refined young lady, Andrea, but you *do* display an unmistakable air of confidence."

He grew quiet, as if he had not intended to say all this. Then he cleared his throat and glanced up at the clock. "It's nearly time to ring the bell."

Mr. Foster's words had thrown Andi into confusion. She didn't know if he was criticizing her family or complimenting them.

"Andrea?"

Andi swallowed her disappointment. "Yes, sir?"

"If I went along with your request, how do you think Marcella would feel?"

Andi studied her shoes. "Not very good," she admitted. If Mr. Foster gave in and moved Andi, Macy would sit alone—publicly scorned and isolated. A worse thought followed. Everyone in the classroom would believe Andrea Carter got her way because her brother was on the school board.

This is definitely not turning out well, she thought grimly.

"As a personal favor to me, would you be willing to continue to share your seat with Marcella?" Mr. Foster pleaded. "I'm asking you to try your best to get along with her. I feel that girl desperately needs a friend."

Andi did not want to agree, but how could she say no? For the first time ever, Mr. Foster was speaking to her as a person and not as an errant pupil. He had lowered his rigid mask and showed Andi a different—even uncertain—side of himself. *Maybe Mr. Foster is afraid of Macy too.*

"I'll give it the ol' Carter try," she said lightly. But inside she was trembling.

Mr. Foster flashed Andi a warm, friendly smile. "Thank you." He stood up and extended his hand across the desk. Andi took it gingerly, uncertain how to react to this new attitude in her usually stern and inflexible teacher. She allowed him to shake her hand, then dropped it to her side when he let go. "Well," he said, "I'd best go ring the bell."

He left Andi gazing after him in wonder and doubt. Did Mr. Foster really believe she wouldn't let Macy make her life miserable? That she had some kind of *confidence*? Shaking her head, she made her way to the desk she shared with the new girl. *I've never felt less confident about anything in my life.*

Andi flopped into her seat. She took the primer from her skirt pocket and set it on Macy's desk in plain sight. Chances were good the new girl would see it, toss it across the room in a fit of rage, and light into Andi for insulting her.

Andi closed her eyes and sent a quick prayer heavenward that she and Macy would not be expelled on the same day.

CHAPTER 10

How can you be a friend to someone who doesn't want to be your friend?

The school bell clanged, bringing a stampede of students into the classroom. There were grins from a number of the boys when they saw Andi seated at her desk. They pinched their noses and sniggered behind their hands. A few young ladies wore expressions of sympathy for Andi's predicament.

"How will you ever endure sitting with that new girl?" Patricia asked. She waved a handkerchief in front of her nose. "I came prepared today. I can smell her from where I sit, and that's clear across the room from you."

"I'll manage," Andi replied stiffly.

"I suppose it comes easier for you, living on a ranch and all," Virginia added from Patricia's side. "That's probably why Father assigned her to you. You're used to all kinds of vicious smells."

"That's all *you* know," Andi replied crossly. "Go sit down before Macy hears you saying such mean things."

"Mean?" Virginia's eyes opened wide. "I wasn't being unkind on purpose." She leaned over, and her voice dropped to a whisper. "I don't want to say anything too loudly, but as your friend, I should warn you that people like her sometimes carry . . . well . . . infestations of the most unpleasant kind."

Andi clenched her fists tightly in her lap. She'd already considered that loathsome possibility. "Virginia . . ." she warned quietly.

"My cousin Bonnie had to wash her hair in kerosene," Patricia chimed in. "When that didn't work, Aunt Priscilla had to cut Bonnie's hair off to get rid of the vermin." She shook her head. "She had beautiful hair, Andi. Just like yours."

Andi fingered the ends of her two thick, dark braids. She didn't want to believe Patricia, yet she had heard similar stories before.

"Outta my way, rich girl!" Macy's loud, surly voice sent Patricia scurrying to her seat in panic. Virginia fled right behind her.

Macy snatched the white square of cloth from Patricia's hand as she passed. She held it to her nose and blew into it. "You don't want it back now, do you, Miss Prissy?" she sneered. She waved the handkerchief like a flag of victory and stuffed it in the back pocket of her overalls.

Andi pressed her lips tightly together to keep from snickering. As uncouth as Macy acted, Andi couldn't help thinking, *Good for you.* Patricia put on airs much too often.

Macy slid into the seat beside Andi just as the tardy bell rang. She propped her chin in her hands and stared straight ahead as though preparing herself for battle. Her elbow slid against the primer. The movement caught her eye.

Macy's brow furrowed. She cast a quick glance around the room then reached out and picked up the primer. She opened it to the first page, where the alphabet was printed in large, dark type.

Andi ignored Mr. Foster's dull announcements and watched her seatmate from the corner of her eye. For a moment, Macy's face lost its tough mask. Her eyes opened wide in interest. Then *bang!* She slammed the book shut and sat back. She nudged Andi. "Where'd this come from? Some fool makin' fun of me, thinkin' I need this baby book?"

At least she hadn't tossed it across the room. "You have to start someplace," Andi said quietly. "You told the teacher that you hadn't been in school long enough to learn to read. I was trying to be nice."

"I don't care about folks being nice to me," Macy snapped. "I ain't here to be nice to anybody or for anybody to be nice to me. I'm here 'cause my brother's makin' me come. That's all. I don't wanna learn nothin' 'less it's how to shoot, ride, and play a mean game o' cards."

"That's all, huh? Well, the book's here now. It can't hurt to learn what's in it." Andi paused. "If you want, I can show you what the letters stand for."

There. She'd done it. She'd made the Macy-needs-a-friend gesture that Mr. Foster had asked of her. If Macy said yes, Andi would follow through, even if she had to plug her nose the entire time. However, if Macy rejected the offer, Andi was off the hook. She held her breath and waited for Macy's response.

Macy sat in stiff silence as though pondering the offer. She started blinking. "Dratted dust," she mumbled and swiped the back of her hand across her eyes. The next instant, her mask fell firmly back into place. "Listen, goody girl. Nobody does me or my kin any favors. I ain't about to be beholdin' to nobody in this hoity-toity town, 'specially not to *you*."

She slid the primer in front of Andi. Then she flung open the cover of her desk and whipped out a slate. "Here's your slate too. I'll use the one in my desk." She pulled out Rosa's old slate and slammed the lid down with a bang.

Andi felt like she'd been punched in the stomach. Macy had hurled her act of kindness back in her face. Angry and disgusted, she watched Macy spit on the slate and wipe it clean with the handkerchief she'd stolen from Patricia. *I can't stay here. Macy's just plain mean. And crude. Mr. Foster is wrong. I can't manage her. Nobody can.*

"What are *you* gawkin' at, Miss Fancy Face?" Macy puckered her lips to launch another round of spittle. For a horrible instant, Andi thought Macy might spit on *her*. Not for Mr. Foster or for her mother or for all the gold in California would Andi sit by and let that happen. *I'll let myself get expelled first*, she decided, her temper rising to full flame. *Mother will just have to understand.*

The thought of her mother kept Andi's fury from spilling over. Instead of shoving Macy away, she wondered what her mother would do in a similar situation. Elizabeth Carter was always an example of graciousness, no matter what unexpected situation she found herself in. But she never gave an inch. How did she do it? More than anything, Andi wanted to be like her mother. More often than not, though, she found herself losing her temper like her brother Chad.

Like right now.

Andi glanced up. Mr. Foster was gazing at her with interest. He'd no doubt seen and heard the girls' conversation. Who could miss it? Macy had not whispered her nasty remarks. The entire class was probably waiting on pins and needles for Act Two, when the new girl would go after her seatmate and both pupils would be expelled.

It was clear the schoolmaster was also waiting for something to happen. He had not yet called the class to Bible reading. He stood quietly in front of his desk with his arms folded across his chest, watching to see how the drama would play out.

Macy seemed unaware of the tension in the air. She had returned to her task of spitting on the slate and rubbing it with the hankie.

Andi took a deep, silent breath and decided to overlook Macy's rude comments. *I can do all things through Christ*, she told herself firmly. *I can get through this too.* She clasped her hands, rested them on top of her desk, and gave the schoolmaster a halfhearted smile. *I'm just not sure how long I can keep it up.*

CHAPTER 11

Melinda likes to think she's as good at
handing out advice as Mother. Maybe she is.
I listen to her only because I'm pretty sure
Mother would say the same thing, and I don't
want to hear it twice.

"Have you had a chance to talk to Mother about Macy?" Melinda asked two days later. She unlatched the gate and entered the pasture, where Andi was working with her colts.

Andi shook her head and continued to brush Shasta. The little colt stood quietly, clearly enjoying the strokes of the brush and the loving attention he was receiving. He nibbled the small piece of apple Melinda offered him.

"Mother's got enough on her mind, thanks to Chad," Andi said. She dropped the brush on the ground and grabbed a hoof pick. "I'm tired of hearing the count of missing cattle every night at supper. I wish the boys would just stay out on the range. Why come home at all if they're just going to grumble and complain at every meal?"

Melinda laughed. "I'm sure it will come to that sooner or later. And I say, the sooner the better."

Andi drew alongside Shasta. "I'm going to pick up your foot, so stand still," she warned her colt. Sliding her hand firmly along Shasta's front leg, she gave him the signal to lift his foot.

"He obeys well," Melinda said. "You've been working hard on his training."

"Nothing annoys Jake more than a skittish horse during shoeing," Andi replied, scraping the pick along the colt's hoof. "I heard him scorch Diego last week when he had to replace a shoe." She cringed at the memory. Diego's horse had danced all over the place, just missing the ranch's farrier with a swift kick. "My colts are never going to give Jake trouble."

"How are things going with Macy?" Melinda asked. "Would you like to talk about it?"

Andi dropped Shasta's foot and straightened up. She gave her older sister a suspicious look. Melinda sounded just like Mother. "Nothing's changed. Why do you want to know?"

Melinda stroked Shasta's nose. "I'm sorry my suggestion about switching seats didn't work. I'm wondering if my hold-on-till-school's-out idea is working any better. Is Macy settling in?"

"She's settling in all right," Andi said with a bitter laugh. "She's the terror of the schoolyard. Miss Hall's pupils scatter like frightened chicks whenever they see her coming. Cory has another black eye to match the one Macy gave him the first day. She stole Ollie's bat and hid it, so now the boys can't play baseball. We played Ante Over until she grabbed the ball and ran off with it."

Andi stopped and took a breath. "Let's see, what else? Oh, yes. Today, she pulled a knife from her pocket and cut the jump rope into a dozen pieces. None of the boys can bring their marbles anymore because she steals them."

Melinda gasped her surprise. "She's done all of that her first week? Why doesn't Mr. Foster do anything?"

"Because he doesn't know about it. Nobody will snitch on her."

"Why not, for goodness' sake?"

"If anybody gets Macy in trouble with the schoolmaster, she says she'll sic her three big brothers on them." Andi leaned against a fence post and let the hoof pick drop to the ground. "I believe her, Melinda. I saw one of her brothers on Macy's first day of school. He dragged her up the stairs and dumped her in the classroom. He was scary mean."

She shuddered. "He hit Macy and threatened to whip her if she didn't stay put. The boys saw him too. I don't blame them for not wanting to tangle with such dangerous men." Andi sighed. "You know what? For the first time in my life, I wish Johnny Wilson was still around, instead of in that military school his father shipped him off to back East."

"You wish the bully was back? After all the misery he caused you last fall?"

Andi nodded. "You bet I do! Johnny could have tamed Macy, and I would have cheered him for doing it. I don't think he would have been scared of her brothers either, big and bold as Johnny is."

Melinda frowned. "So Macy's running the school?"

"The schoolyard, anyway."

"Is she learning anything in class?"

"I don't think so," Andi admitted. "Although the primer I left for her is gone. She probably took it home and used the pages to start a fire." She shrugged. "Maybe she'll burn down whatever shack she's staying in, and she and her brothers will get run out of town. And good riddance."

"That was unkind," Melinda scolded her. "Didn't Mr. Foster tell you Macy needs a friend? It doesn't sound like you're trying very hard."

Andi scowled. She was sorry she'd shared what had happened. Melinda wasn't in the classroom. She didn't know how miserable things were, especially for Andi, who—thanks to her family's reputation for "coping"—had to sit with Macy seven long hours a day. *It's time this conversation ended.*

She tugged on her colt's lead rope and turned away. "Macy doesn't need a friend," she muttered under her breath. "She needs a prison matron."

"Andi!" Melinda sounded shocked. "You don't mean that."

Yes, I do. Only, she hadn't intended for Melinda to hear that last remark. Her words had tumbled out before she could stop them.

"What's happening in the schoolyard can't go on," Melinda continued.

"One of the little children might get hurt. Somebody has to let the schoolmaster know."

"It's not going to be me," Andi called over her shoulder and kept walking.

Melinda hurried to catch up. "Why not? You're her seatmate. The other kids are probably watching to see what you'll do."

Andi stopped. Shasta stopped. Sunny nibbled at Andi's hair. "Why? Because I'm a *Carter*?"

Melinda nodded.

Andi blew out an angry breath and pushed her colt away. Being part of an important family had its downsides. "Just because she sits next to me doesn't make her my responsibility."

"Doesn't it?" Melinda asked. "What she's doing is wrong. She needs to recognize that she cannot act like an outlaw. Someone needs to help that poor girl become a better person." A slight flush rose to her cheeks.

My tenderhearted and idealistic big sister is really torn up over Macy, Andi thought. Which seemed ridiculous, since Melinda had never met her. *Maybe she should take my place in class and heal all of Macy's hurts in one afternoon.*

Andi wanted to snap out her thoughts, but she sighed instead. "Melinda, please. You sound just like Mother."

Melinda laughed and relaxed. "Thank you. I guess I'm feeling awfully sorry for Macy."

"I feel sorry for the rest of us."

"But don't you see?" Melinda's eyes shone with a zeal Andi didn't feel. "Macy is all broken up inside. She's sad and lonely. She must hate herself so much that she hates everybody else too. Can't you show her a little bit of God's love by trying to be her friend?"

Andi pulled on Shasta's lead rope and urged her forward. "Do you think I haven't tried? Macy doesn't want to be friends."

To tell the truth, she hadn't tried very hard to make friends. Especially not since yesterday, when Macy had sneaked up from behind and poured the entire bucket of drinking water over Andi's head during afternoon recess. She heard the warning cry from Cory an instant too late.

The soaking would not have been bad—quite refreshing actually—if Macy had removed the dipper first. As it happened, Andi's cheek now sported a painful bruise from the long-handled, metal dipper. Fortunately, the sun had dried Andi enough that Mr. Foster didn't notice her damp clothes when he called them inside.

Or did he? Andi suddenly wasn't sure what Mr. Foster was thinking. Maybe he knew about the schoolyard incidents and was content to bury his head in the sand and wait for the term to end. There were only a few short weeks left. *No fair!* The schoolmaster always brought unruly students swiftly to justice. Why not now?

"Be Macy's friend," Melinda pleaded, breaking into Andi's thoughts. "You can start by keeping her from hurting others. Let her know you're not going to stand by quietly and let her keep terrorizing the schoolyard. Tell Mr. Foster what's going on. Show Macy you care enough to help her find a better way."

Andi shook her head. "I don't think I care enough, big sister." She unbuckled her colts' halters and gave them a friendly slap on their rumps. Shasta scampered off to join the others under the shade trees, with Sunny right behind him.

When she turned around, she saw Melinda's imploring look and gave in. "All right, Melinda. I'll consider it." Her stomach turned over at the idea of standing up to Macy. "I'll try to show Macy I care about her, but it won't be easy." She gave her sister a crooked smile. "If Macy's brothers come after me, you better send Chad and Mitch to my rescue."

Melinda hugged her. "I promise."

CHAPTER 12

Everyone says "advice is cheap," but that's not true. Advice is expensive, especially when I'm the one trying to follow it.

"I can't take it much longer," Cory grumbled, coming up beside Andi during Friday noon recess. Macy had chased him down and stolen his dinner pail right out of his hands. "She's only been here five days, and the entire school is suffering." He clenched a fist at Macy's retreating back. "If she wasn't a girl, I'd settle this so fast her head would spin."

"Sure you would," Andi said, unconvinced. "Boy or girl, you'd still have Macy's brothers to contend with." At fifteen, Cory was tall and strong, but he was no match for a trio of mean men. "If you try to tame Macy, I *suppose* I could lend you Chad or Mitch," she teased. Then she shrugged. "But the boys are caught up with rustler problems, and you can't fight a girl—not even an especially nasty one."

"Mr. Foster would take a piece of my hide for sure," Cory agreed. "Then Pa would finish the job." He tugged on Andi's sleeve. "Uh, what if . . ." He paused and cleared his throat. "What if *you* stood up to her?"

Andi winced. Cory's words echoed Melinda's.

"We think you could—"

"Who are 'we'?" Andi whirled on him. "Does the whole class think it's up to me?"

Cory looked sheepish. He nodded.

"I don't want to stand up to a roughneck, trouble-making girl who's looking for an excuse to hurt somebody," Andi said. "Besides, I don't want to draw her brothers' attention any more than you do."

"If *you* stood up to her, I think she'd back down," Cory said. He looked at her. "Listen, Andi. If Macy was a boy, I'd do it, brothers or not." When Andi smirked her disbelief, Cory scowled. "Yes, I would! You're the only girl in the classroom with enough grit to go up against her. Everybody's counting on you, even Patricia. She's riled because Macy stole her handkerchief. She wants it back."

Andi wrinkled her nose. "I wouldn't want it. Not after Macy used it." The last thing she wanted to do was confront Macy Walker. She didn't care how many friends were counting on her. It seemed even Mr. Foster was waiting for something. His words from the other day haunted her. *"You won't let her."*

The schoolmaster was wrong. Andi *had* let Macy make her life miserable. She sighed. Maybe the time had come. A huge cloud had settled over the classroom this past week.

"I'll stick close by," Cory promised. "If she takes a swing at you, I'll . . . I'll . . ." His voice trailed off.

"You'll *protect* me?" Andi crooned, batting her eyelashes at him. "Like my knight in shining armor?" With satisfaction she watched Cory's face turn bright red. *That should teach him to wink at me during arithmetic.*

"Aw, Andi," Cory said. "Leave off. I only meant—"

A sharp wail interrupted their conversation. The little girls from Miss Hall's primary class sat under a tree, playing tea party with their dolls. Macy was pestering them. "What about standing up to Macy to look out for the younger kids?" Cory asked.

Cindy's sobs made Andi's fists clench. "All right. For Cindy." She took a deep breath and started toward the group. It was hard to keep her temper reined in. Macy held Cindy's porcelain doll over her head and was roughing up the delicate clothes.

"Crybaby, crybaby!" Macy gave Cindy a rough shove, which sent the little girl sprawling. She howled. Macy twirled the precious doll over her head and laughed.

A fire lit inside Andi's belly. She understood how a little boy might behave in such a spiteful way. Her young nephew, Levi, had been just as mean at one time—stealing marbles and acting out his anger by picking fights.

But Macy? She was close to Andi's age and almost grown up. Why would she pick on such a small child? What was *wrong* with her?

"Macy! Stop it!" Andi hollered and hurried over. Cory stuck to her side as promised.

A hush fell over the schoolyard. All eyes turned toward the oak tree. Andi blushed at the spectacle she was making of herself. Or was it from fury? Either way, her cheeks flamed.

Cindy jumped up and threw her arms around Andi's waist. Tears streamed down her face. "Make her give me my dolly. Please! She's hurting her." Cindy choked and blubbered, clutching Andi like a lifeline. "Grandmama gave her to me last Christmas."

Andi hugged Cindy and took a shaky breath to keep the red-hot fire in her gut from exploding. She'd felt it plenty of times before. *Temper, temper, little sister*, Chad often teased, when he clearly had his own battles to fight against anger and impatience.

This time was different. Something deep inside told Andi it was all right to be furious at Macy for hurting Cindy. It was right to stand up to the bullying, just so long as she didn't lose her temper and fly into Macy like she'd flown into Virginia that long-ago day.

She forced herself to speak quietly. "Macy, please give Cindy her doll."

Macy snorted. "Make me."

The girls stared at each other. Cory stepped closer. Andi's heart pounded at the challenge. She wanted nothing more than to "make her." She wouldn't. Not today. "Sarah, run and get Mr. Foster," she said.

The little girls gasped. Sarah jumped up to do Andi's bidding.

"Squeal, and I'll get you real good," Macy told Sarah. "Right after school."

Sarah looked at Andi, terror in her wide, brown eyes.

"Don't worry about Macy, Sarah. *I'm* telling you to get the teacher. I'm doing the tattling." Andi bored her gaze into Macy's pale eyes. "Isn't that right, Macy?"

Macy's eyes flashed fire.

Sarah ran off quicker than a jackrabbit. As soon as the little girl disappeared around the corner of the schoolhouse, Macy exploded. "You ain't gonna make me? You gonna *squeal* instead?"

Andi's throat felt drier than dust. "Mr. Foster will handle this."

"You're scared of me, ain't ya? Just like all the rest. 'Fraidy-cat," she jeered.

Andi said nothing. The longer she stood still, the easier it became to shove her anger into a corner. *Yes, I'm afraid. But I won't let on to Macy.* "You aren't worth getting expelled over. And if I light into you, I *will* get expelled." So would Macy, but Andi had no desire to become the class's sacrificial lamb. Not with only three weeks of school left.

Macy's mouth dropped open, and her pale face reddened. She dropped the doll. It fell to the ground with a soft *thunk* of its china head.

Cindy rushed over and snatched up her doll. She turned shining eyes on Andi. "Thank you, thank you! I knew you could do it."

Andi's hands shook, but all she could think was, *Cory was right. I stood up to Macy and she backed down. Melinda was right too.* When she looked at Cory, he nodded. "I told you," he said.

At that moment, Sarah and Mr. Foster ran up. Andi's eyes grew wide. The schoolmaster was *running*. Sarah's report must have fired him up. "What seems to be the trouble?" he asked, panting. He pulled out a handkerchief and mopped his brow.

"No trouble, sir." Andi smiled at Macy. "It's all settled, isn't it?" *Say yes, Macy, or you're gonna catch it from Mr. Foster.*

"Not by a long shot, it ain't."

Mr. Foster beckoned Cindy to his side. "Have you been crying, Cynthia?"

Cindy wiped her eyes and looked up at the teacher. "That *horrible* Macy took my doll and pushed me down and—"

"Be still, Cindy," Andi warned.

Cindy clearly had no intention of keeping silent about her heroine, especially when she was standing safely at Mr. Foster's side. "Andi rescued my doll and made Macy give it back."

"It was just a misunderstanding," Andi said quickly. If Macy agreed, the schoolmaster would most likely send everybody back to class. He looked unwilling to stir up "Macy" trouble this afternoon.

Macy snorted. "Wasn't no misunderstanding. I wanted the doll and the kid wouldn't give it to me. So I took it." She jammed her hands on her hips. "Whatcha gonna do about it, Teacher?"

By now, the rest of the pupils had wandered over to watch the standoff between their teacher and the new girl. *You nitwit!* Andi thought. Mr. Foster couldn't ignore an outright challenge to his authority. Not even Johnny the bully ever dared to smart off openly to the schoolmaster.

Mr. Foster straightened to his full height, took a deep breath, and pronounced judgment. "Marcella Walker, I have been patient with you this first week of school. I know you are new and feeling out of sorts. But I cannot overlook your impudence or this act of cruelty against Cindy. I must punish you."

Macy laughed and held out her hand. "Here's my palm. Smack away."

"The time for the ruler is past."

Macy paled. Before she could dart away, Mr. Foster had her by the wrist and was pulling her toward the schoolhouse. Macy turned into a wildcat, but the schoolmaster held on. "I'll ring the bell in a minute," he called back to his gaping students.

"I'll get you for this, Andi," Macy shrieked. "You dirty, squealin' *pig!*"

"She's bluffing," Cory said, but Andi knew better. She steeled herself for a long afternoon session.

Not a sound came from the schoolroom the rest of the day. Surprisingly, Macy did nothing to annoy Andi. Red-faced and muttering under her breath, she sat perfectly still and stared at her desktop. She didn't look at Andi. She didn't look at anyone else either. When Mr. Foster dismissed class, she tore down the steps and out the door. From the upstairs window, Andi saw her disappear toward the center of town. *Good riddance.*

Andi felt nothing but relief that the school day was over and she could go home. Compared to putting up with Macy, Chad's heated accounts of cattle rustlers sounded tranquil. She filed soberly out of the room and down the steps with the rest of the students.

"What did I tell you, Andi?" Cory remarked when they gathered in the schoolyard. "You stood up to her, and she backed down. Macy will give us no more trouble."

A dozen other grateful pupils expressed their gratitude.

Virginia let out a deep sigh of relief. "I, for one, am certainly glad *that's* over."

Andi shook her head. "You're wrong, all of you. I think it's barely begun."

CHAPTER 13

*Perhaps I should play hooky from school for
the rest of the term. It would be a blessed
relief. Mr. Blake might let me clean out his livery
stable during the day. Justin wouldn't catch me;
he's not in town. He's too busy chasing cattle-
rustling "ghosts." I ride to town in the morning
by myself, and I return home every afternoon.
Mother would never know.*

*I think a journal can sometimes read like
a work of fiction.*

Andi made her way down Ventura Street alone, deep in thought. Her friends had praised her courage, but Andi did not feel brave. She felt tired. Would Macy's behavior change overnight just because somebody had stood up to her? Not likely.

Andi turned the corner and continued down K Street until the livery came into view. "Everything will look better after a good, fast ride home on Taffy," she told herself. "And I have two whole days to work with the colts." Her spirits rose. "Maybe I'll ride up to my special spot."

The *clop, clop, clop* of nearby hooves brought Andi out of her weekend planning. She looked up. A shiny black, two-seated buggy rolled to a stop along the sidewalk. "Andi!" a cheerful voice called to her.

"Howdy, Lucy." Andi wondered—not for the first time—why Justin and Lucy hadn't set a wedding date. Still, she was glad they were taking their time. She didn't want to lose Justin just yet. Who would help smooth things over with Mother if Andi's oldest and favorite brother was not around? Who would step in and take her side when she and Chad clashed? *Take as much time as you like, big brother. Maybe somebody else will sweep Lucy off her feet while you're dillydallying.*

Andi knew her thoughts were silly and little-girl selfish. Everybody grew up, and most folks got married. It was as inevitable as the rising sun, and it wasn't like Justin was rushing into it. No sirree! He was thirty years old—nearly an old man.

Andi could not find one legitimate reason for not liking her brother's choice for a wife, except that she was from the city. Andi was wise enough not to air her prejudice out loud. The stranger-from-San-Francisco objection would never fly with Justin. Besides, Lucy lived in Fresno now and kept house for her brother, an up-and-coming young lawyer. Her whole family was delighted with the prospect of their daughter marrying Justin Carter.

Right now, the future Mrs. Justin Carter looked completely at ease driving the lively bay horse. She brushed a wayward strand of dark-brown hair from her face and said, "I saw Mitch in town earlier. He thought Justin might like it if I surprised him and rode out to the ranch for supper." She smiled, and dimples cut into both cheeks. "I heard he's missing town these days."

"You heard right," Andi said. "He's had enough of standing night watches and listening to Chad rant about rustlers." She giggled. "He says it's worse than putting up with a hostile witness in court. He misses his quiet, tidy law office." She smiled up at Lucy. "Mostly, though, I think he misses seeing *you*."

Lucy's cheeks turned pink. "I'm on my way out to the ranch. Would you like a ride?"

Andi shook her head. "The colts are being weaned, so I've been riding

Taffy to town the past couple of weeks. Mother had a long talk with Mr. Foster about allowing me to wear a split skirt so I could ride astride." She looked down at her dark-brown outfit. "He gave his permission, though grudgingly."

"You could tie Taffy up behind the buggy," Lucy urged.

Andi felt torn. Lucy clearly wanted company for the hour-long drive out to the ranch. *I don't want to talk. I want to ride.* She backed away from the buggy. "Thanks, Lucy, but I've had a bad day. I need to ride it out."

"I understand." The barest hint of disappointment colored Lucy's voice. "I'll see you at the ranch."

Andi grinned. "I bet I beat you there."

"If you do, don't tell Justin I'm coming. I want to surprise him."

"I promise." Andi hurried to the livery. To her surprise, she found Taffy saddled, bridled, and tied up outside, ready to go. Cory's father had a heart of gold. He'd taken time out of his busy afternoon to saddle her horse.

Andi circled Taffy and checked the cinch and stirrups. She could have saved herself the trouble. Mr. Blake had done his usual thorough job. "Thanks, Mr. Blake!" she called into the livery stable's dark opening.

When he didn't answer, Andi unwrapped the reins and led her horse into the street. She shaded her eyes and looked around for Lucy's rig. It was nowhere in sight. "She must really be missing Justin," she told Taffy. "She sure disappeared fast."

Andi put her foot in the stirrup and hoisted herself up. She couldn't wait to feel the hot afternoon wind whip across her face. "Come on, Taffy. We'll catch her in no time." Eager to be on her way, Andi slammed down hard in the saddle and felt around for the other stirrup.

Her foot never made it.

Taffy screamed and reared. Andi instinctively doubled over to keep her seat. The saddle horn jabbed her stomach and made her gasp. The next instant, Taffy's front hooves hit the ground. She bolted—streaking down K Street like a shot out of last summer's Fourth of July cannon.

Andi snatched at the reins. She'd lost them at Taffy's surprise move; they dangled alongside the mare's neck, useless. Even if she managed to grab them, Andi doubted she could bring Taffy under control. She felt as if she were clinging to a runaway train engine. Sawing at her horse's mouth would accomplish nothing.

Andi reached out a shaky hand and stroked her mare's neck. "What's wrong, girl? Simmer down. It's all righ—"

Taffy jumped over a small peddler's cart in the middle of the street and swerved to the left without a break in her frenzied pace. Andi's neck snapped in a painful jerk. She clutched Taffy's mane to keep from slipping off and tried to feel for the stirrup with her right foot. It slapped against her horse's side, out of reach.

Two blocks rushed by in a blur. Through watering eyes, Andi watched people scramble out of the way. "Runaway!" somebody hollered.

Andi hung on tighter, wishing she'd let Taffy dump her when she'd had the chance. She could have slid off during those first few seconds when Taffy reared. It was better to be sitting in the dusty street mortified than to be scared senseless.

Taffy raced on. Off to the right, the tree-lined Courthouse Park came into view. Taffy made a beeline for the trees and tried to scrape her rider off under each one. Andi pressed her head into Taffy's neck and stayed low.

Horse and rider broke out of the park and headed north toward the river. Taffy acted crazed, trying to escape from an invisible pain she could not outrun. For two full miles she held to that killing pace. Panic welled up inside Andi. *She's going to run herself to death!* She kept one hand rubbing Taffy's neck and tried soft-talking.

It did no good.

Andi had never been afraid on the back of a horse, not even when she was racing Taffy breakneck across the valley. But she was afraid now—afraid for herself and afraid for her horse. Taffy could run like the wind, but she'd never before run so hard and fast that she might *break* her wind. She was blowing badly.

Fresno fell farther behind. Taffy's pace never lessened. Whatever was driving the mare clearly had her in its grip. What would happen when they reached the river? Would Taffy plow straight into it? Andi shivered and choked back a sob. She did not want to drown.

Just then, Andi heard a yell and the sound of hoofbeats above Taffy's. She hazarded a glance over her shoulder. A handful of riders were racing after her. One horse and rider galloped far ahead of the others. The shout of "runaway" must have mustered a few hardy souls from town to attempt a rescue. *Oh, hurry!* she pleaded silently to the lead rider.

A sudden jolt dislodged Andi's foot from the remaining stirrup and nearly threw her from the saddle. She saw the flash of an old, barbed-wire fence and felt herself sailing over the top. Taffy hit the ground without slowing down, jarring Andi into the air and almost over her mare's head.

With the stirrups useless, Andi stayed in the saddle by clinging to Taffy's neck like a leech. Her arms ached, but she kept her numbing grip. One more jump like that—or even a stumble—and she would somersault off her horse and onto the ground. Andi squeezed her eyes shut and prayed the rider would catch up.

The hammering hooves drew nearer. A voice shouted at her, but she couldn't make out the words over the roaring in her ears and Taffy's ragged breathing. Through eyes half shut, Andi saw a sorrel horse galloping closer. *Chase!* Relief surged through her. Mitch and Chase always won a match race against Taffy. If anybody could catch her, Mitch could.

Chase's presence had a calming effect on Taffy. The mare slowed from a killing gallop to a swinging lope. Mitch and Chase matched Taffy's stride pace for pace. "Hang on, Andi. Be ready!" her brother yelled.

Andi nodded. She hoped Mitch would snag the flapping reins and slow Taffy down, but he didn't even try. He dropped Chase's reins, leaned far over, and grabbed Andi around the waist. With a jerk that forced the air from her lungs, Mitch yanked her onto his horse and kept galloping. Soon he slowed Chase to a trot, then to a walk, and finally brought his horse to a complete stop.

"You can let go now." Mitch was breathing hard; so was Chase. But the sorrel gelding tossed his head and snorted as if he were just getting started on a good run.

Andi clung tighter to her brother. She planned to stay like that until she recovered her wits—which would not be any time soon. She was shaking too hard.

Mitch peeled Andi's arms away and dropped her off his horse. He joined her on the ground, where she'd collapsed into a limp, quivering heap. "The way you took off, I reckoned you'd soon be in Oregon," he said, grinning. "That was quite a ride. You're white as chalk."

Andi's throat felt too tight to talk. She burst into tears.

Mitch reached out and drew her close. Then he patted her back, just like he used to do when she was little. "It's all right, Sis. You're safe now. I've got you."

At that moment, the other riders from town pulled up. They looked relieved to see the chase had ended. "Are you all right, Miss Carter?" One of the men pulled out a bandana and dabbed at his sweaty face. "That fence was quite a leap for this old cowboy."

Andi swiped a hand across her wet cheeks and nodded.

"Good thing Mitch was in town. He was runnin' for his horse before you'd gone three blocks. Don't think we'd have caught up. Never seen nothin' like it, the way your horse took off." He laughed and pointed at Chase. "Mitch Carter, if you sign up to ride that horse in the Fourth of July race this year, I'm withdrawing."

Andi managed a polite smile, but she didn't feel like laughing. She wished the riders would go back to town and leave Mitch and her alone.

"Thanks, fellas." Mitch raised a hand and waved them off.

"No need for thanks," another rider offered. "A runaway is dangerous. Of course we'd follow and do what we could." He tipped his hat and rode away.

"I heard somebody yell 'runaway,'" Mitch said a minute later. "When I saw it was you and Taffy, my heart nearly stopped. Speaking of your horse . . ." He looked around.

"There she is." Andi pointed toward a clump of valley oaks about fifty yards away. Once Andi had left her back, Taffy had settled down. Now she stood under the trees waiting. Andi tried to whistle, but her fingers shook. No sound came out of her dust-dry mouth.

"Let me," Mitch said. At his shrill whistle, Taffy turned her head and gave an answering whinny. Then she trotted over, acting as if nothing had happened during the past wild minutes. She came up alongside Chase and stood quietly. The mare's sides still heaved, but she was no longer fighting for each lungful of air.

Andi didn't understand it. Why had Taffy panicked and run away? She shuddered when she thought how close she had come to—

"It's over now, Sis," Mitch reminded her. He stood and reached down to give her a hand up. "Come on. Let's go home."

Sudden suspicion crept into Andi's gut, propelling her to her feet without Mitch's help. All weariness fled. "It's *not* over." She ran to Taffy.

"What are you talking about?" Mitch followed her. "Be careful. She may still be spooked."

"You can see for yourself that she's fine." Andi patted Taffy's nose. "Aren't you, girl?" She loosened the girth and let the saddle and blanket fall to the ground. The mare's golden coat was dark with sweat. "You'll need an extra-good rubdown today."

"What are you doing?" Mitch asked.

Andi didn't answer. She overturned the saddle, smoothed out the blanket, and began a careful search. Something had caused Taffy to bolt when Andi sat down in the saddle. A thorn? A burr? She intended to find out what it was.

Her search was rewarded in less than a minute.

Andi sucked in a sharp breath. This was no burr or thorn, but a deliberately set tack. Its long, silvery point gleamed when she plucked it from the blanket. Andi held it up, dumbstruck. Set just under the saddle, the slightest weight would punch the tack through the saddle blanket and into Taffy's back.

Mitch's mouth fell open. "What in the world?"

"It's a tack," Andi whispered, dropping it into her brother's hand. "And I know who put it there." She grabbed Taffy's mane, pulled herself onto her bare back, and reached for the reins.

"Hold it right there. Where are you going?"

Andi didn't answer. She didn't even look back.

CHAPTER 14

Life would go a lot smoother for me if I could only remember to stop and think before I plunge headlong into things.

Andi did not push her horse on the four-mile ride back to town, although she wanted to arrive before Mitch caught up. She consoled herself with the fact that he would have to cool Chase down too. Plus, she hoped he would lug her saddle back with him. The delay would give Andi a chance to finish what she set out to do.

By the time the courthouse dome came into view, Andi was breathing fire. "She's gone too far," she told Taffy. "Schoolyard mischief is one thing, but hurting *you* is . . ." She couldn't think of a word bad enough to describe Macy's cruelty. "Nobody hurts my horse," she fumed. "I'll find her and I'll—"

You'll do what? The unspoken question slipped into Andi's mind. It startled her, and she pulled back on the reins. Taffy slowed to a jarring trot, which rattled Andi's nerves more. "I'll show her she can't get away with doing vicious things like that."

How? By knocking her down? Come on, Andrea. Haven't you learned anything?

"Sure I have." She'd reined in her temper earlier today, but . . . "This is different," she insisted. Andi did not like the mental seesaw on which she found herself. She wanted to shake some sense into Macy and hurt her the way Andi had been hurt and scared. Her stomach was tied in knots from her terrifying ride.

"Why shouldn't I give Macy what she deserves? Nobody else will." Even Mr. Foster had encouraged Andi to manage Macy. "I'll *manage* her, all right," she said.

Be angry and sin not.

Andi cringed. Why did Bible verses pop into her head at the most awkward times? She was angry, and she intended to *stay* angry. It was the only way to keep from dissolving into tears at the thought of what could have happened to her and Taffy if Mitch had not shown up.

Andi looked up and down K Street for the girl who had acted so wickedly. In her eyes, Macy Walker was only one step short of a murderess. If Macy knew what was good for her, she'd find a deep hole to hide in. She surely wouldn't dare show her face in school on Monday.

"It will be worth the ride if she doesn't return to class," Andi convinced herself when she'd searched two other streets. She prodded Taffy into a faster trot and turned onto Front Street near the railroad tracks. If she rode quickly, she could check for Macy near the town's most frequented saloons and be gone before Mitch tracked her down.

Five minutes later Andi found her.

Macy was leaning against a post in front of the Diamond Drink saloon, idly watching the street traffic of wagons, horses, and buggies go by. When she saw Andi, her pale-blue eyes opened wide. She straightened up and clapped a hand over her mouth. Two red spots colored her cheeks.

Andi didn't know what to think. She'd expected Macy to greet her with a mocking laugh or pretend she knew nothing about the tack. Instead, a look of genuine shock covered her face. It was mixed with the tiniest amount of . . . was it guilt and shame?

Wordlessly, Andi dismounted. She left Taffy ground tied in the dusty street and stepped up on the boardwalk. A slight breeze blew at the wild tangles that had torn loose from her braids. A rush of fury warmed her face. "Macy!" She curled her hands into fists.

Be angry and sin not!

Andi ignored the mental warning and waited for Macy's response.

Macy stood chewing on a dirty thumbnail. She dropped her gaze to the sidewalk. "Have a nice ride?" She scuffed her bare toes across the boards. "You nearly ran my horse to death," Andi said. "That's the meanest thing anybody could ever do, Macy. A tack!"

Macy looked up. A flicker of uncertainty crossed her face. Her eyes looked watery, as if she might cry. She jammed her hands into her pockets and sniffed. "Yeah, I know."

Andi wrinkled her forehead, puzzled. Macy acted sorry. It didn't make sense.

"What's goin' on here?" A man's voice cracked like a rifle shot from behind Macy. Both girls jumped.

Andi glanced past Macy into the eyes of a rough, wild-looking man. Bright red hair covered his head and most of his face. It stuck out all over in tight curls, uncombed and unshaven. He caught Andi staring and leered at her, revealing huge gaps where two or three teeth were missing.

Andi looked away, heart pounding. What did she expect, standing in front of Fresno's most popular saloon? This fellow was probably heading inside, and she and Macy were blocking his way. It was time to go. *If Mitch finds me near this den of iniquity, I'll catch it for sure.*

The stranger reached out a massive hand and closed it around Macy's wrist. She flinched as though slapped. "I asked you a question. What's goin' on?"

"N-nothin', Rudy," Macy stuttered. She looked scared. "Me and this girl got business t' settle, that's all."

Rudy shoved a long hank of hair away from his eyes and squinted at Andi. "That a fact, girl?"

Fear rooted Andi to her spot.

"I think she was fixin' to take a swing at me," Macy said. Her eyes held a trapped look Andi had not noticed earlier.

Rudy burst into coarse laughter. "All righty!" He motioned Andi closer.

"Come and get her." He grasped a handful of Macy's matted hair. "I'll hold m' sister for the first couple o' punches. If ya hurry, she'll be easy to take."

"I'll show ya who's easy!" Macy screeched. She lashed out with her bare feet, but the huge man held her fast. By now, a cluster of Diamond Drink patrons had gathered around. The men lounged against the posts, chuckling at the spectacle. Coins passed between a few of them. No one intervened.

Rudy roared his amusement. "Can't hold this here wildcat much longer. Better get your knocks in while ya can before she makes mincemeat outta ya."

Andi backed away, thoroughly shaken. Her foot caught as she stepped off the boardwalk, and she stumbled to regain her balance. This brute was Macy's brother? Why would he goad her into a fight and put her on public display? It looked like he could hardly wait for the girls to go at one another. The other no-accounts looked just as eager.

"What're ya waitin' for?" Rudy jeered. "She's an ornery little cuss. Pay her back for whatever she did to you. An eye for an eye."

Andi backed farther into the street and reached for Taffy's bridle to steady herself. All her dark anger toward Macy suddenly vanished in the glaring light of this new discovery. She no longer had any wish to return evil for evil. Shame for even considering it flooded her heart. It was clear that Macy already had enough evil in her life. *I am so sorry, God*, Andi prayed. *I didn't understand. Now I do. Please forgive me.*

Coming on the heels of her short prayer, Andi felt a glimmer of compassion for the poor, mistreated girl. At the same time, she thought of a way out of this sorry fix. She patted Taffy and forced a smile. "I came to ask Macy if she'd like to ride my horse."

Macy stopped squirming. She gaped at Andi.

Rudy swore and shoved his sister into the street. She sprawled at Andi's feet. "You had your chance, goody-girl. Go get her, Macy. Show her what's what." The other men cheered.

Andi clutched Taffy's bridle. Panic welled up. *Please protect me, God.*

Macy pulled herself to her feet and studied Andi. Her breath came in frightened gasps.

Andi glanced past Macy at the sorriest excuse for a brother she had ever seen. Then her heart leaped. Like a shining knight from *Ivanhoe*—the book Melinda was currently reading aloud in the evenings—Mitch stood only a few feet behind the huge stranger. A grim but determined expression covered his face.

Andi returned her gaze to Macy. She felt stronger. "Do you want to ride my horse?"

"I . . ." Macy faltered and nodded.

Rudy took two steps forward. "Why, you little—"

Mitch seized Rudy's arm and jerked it up behind his back. Rudy yelped in surprise and pain. "Let the girls be," Mitch suggested softly. "Why don't you go buy yourself a drink?" He nodded at the rowdies idling nearby. "Take your friends with you."

Rudy struggled and swore, but Mitch held him fast. "None of that," he warned. "We don't take kindly to strangers bothering young ladies on the street. You and I should maybe pay a visit to Sheriff Tate."

When none of the bystanders seemed inclined to interfere with Mitch's street justice, Rudy stopped struggling. He clearly wanted no dealings with the sheriff. "You win," he growled.

Mitch released his hold and gave Rudy a shove that sent him staggering through the swinging doors and into the saloon. "Our jail has a fine selection of cells," he called in parting. "Mind your manners or you'll find yourself in one of them." He brushed his hands together in satisfaction and turned to Andi. "You girls go along and enjoy your ride. I have a couple of errands to attend to. I'll meet you at Blake's in, say, half an hour?"

Andi nodded wordlessly. Mitch didn't sound shook up at finding his little sister in front of the Diamond Drink. He said nothing about Andi being in the company of such disreputable men. She wasn't fooled. He was probably saving his scolding for the trip home.

"Well?" Macy's impatient voice cut into Andi's worries. "Are you gonna give me a ride on your horse or not?"

Andi forced a smile. "Sure."

By the time she pulled herself up on Taffy's bare back and helped Macy up behind her, Mitch was tapping his foot impatiently. "Get on out of here," he advised.

Andi prodded Taffy into an easy lope that left Front Street far behind. *Now what?* she wondered dismally. The spark of compassion she'd felt earlier would go out completely if Macy pulled some new trick.

To her relief, Macy said nothing on their jaunt around town. She held firmly to Andi's waist and seemed to enjoy the ride. A silent Macy was a nice change. Andi rode by the train depot and packing houses, across the flats and past the schoolhouse.

Macy broke the silence fifteen minutes later. "You got a good horse."

"Thanks."

Macy took a deep breath then let it out. Her next words came out as a whisper. "You can sure ride. Ain't never seen nobody stay on a horse like you did."

"I didn't have a choice," Andi admitted. "I had to stay on or else . . ." Her voice trailed away. *Don't think about it!*

"I know you won't believe me," Macy said, "but I never meant for you to get so close to dyin'. The minute that ol' horse felt the tack, I knew she'd rear up. You'd tumble into the street and that would be that. I'd get a good laugh and pay you back for the thrashin' I got from the teacher." She sniffed. "When the horse took off with you, I ain't never been so scared."

"Me neither," Andi said with a shaky laugh.

Macy groaned. "I'm tryin' to 'pologize. I saw how mad and scared you were when you got back to town, and I knew I was in for it. You looked riled enough to lick me good. But you didn't. You gave me a ride on your horse instead. How come you didn't wallop me when Rudy gave you the chance?"

Andi fell silent. How could she explain what she hardly understood herself? When she suddenly saw Macy as God saw her—as a trapped, broken person who needed a friend—Andi's anger fizzled away. Melinda had been right all along. Macy *was* hiding a lot of hurts behind her mean mask.

"Gonna answer or not?" Macy demanded.

"When I saw how your brother treated you, God took all my anger away. I didn't want to do anything mean to you anymore." She sighed. "I guess I just wanted to be your friend . . . because it doesn't look like you've got any, not even your own family."

"Ain't *that* the truth," Macy said. "If that young stranger hadn't grabbed Rudy and cooled him down, you and me woulda been in a heap o' trouble. Rudy's got a mean streak a mile wide. He loves fights of all kinds—cockfights, dogfights. Once he pitted a bear against a pack of meaner-than-sin dogs." She shivered. "It was ugly."

Andi had heard of cockfights and other goings-on in the shadier parts of town, but she'd never seen such a thing, and she didn't want to. She would take Macy's word that it was an ugly business. "I was mighty glad when Mitch stepped in too," she said.

"He a friend o' yours?"

"He's my brother," Andi said proudly. "He rescued me north of town when Taffy ran away."

"Lucky for *you*," Macy said. "And for me too. You coulda been killed, and it woulda been my fault." She paused. "Can you . . . well . . . can you ever set aside what I done to you?"

Andi didn't hesitate. "It's finished. Let's forget it."

"Will your brother turn me over to the sheriff?"

"Mitch has more to worry about than mean pranks from a schoolgirl. He's got cattle rustlers on his mind." She looked up at the sky and pulled Taffy around. "I'd best be heading back. Can I drop you somewhere?"

"One place's good as another."

Macy sounded so sad that Andi wanted to cheer her up. Before she changed her mind, she blurted, "Would you like to come out to the ranch sometime and see my colts?"

"You got *colts*?"

"Yep. Twin colts from this mare we're riding. Would you like to see them?"

"You mean it? *Me?*" Macy sounded breathless with disbelief and hope.

Andi twisted around to look Macy straight in the eye. "Yes, I mean it."

"You crazy or somethin'? I just about killed you back there. Why would you invite me to your place to see twin colts?"

"So maybe you'll believe me when I say I really do want to be your friend." Andi lowered Macy to the ground in front of the mercantile. She smiled at her—a smile she did not have to pretend. "And maybe, if you like playing with the colts, you'll want to be *my* friend."

CHAPTER 15

There is nothing better in the whole world than having a family who loves me and watches out for me, even when I make the same mistakes over and over again.

Andi expected a dressing down from her brother for being where she shouldn't, but when she dismounted at the livery, Mitch surprised her. He didn't mention the Diamond Drink or its unsavory patrons. He didn't grumble about hauling her saddle back to town either. He just saddled Taffy and helped Andi mount up.

"I'm not a china doll," she protested. "I won't break. Let's get going."

Mitch kept a firm grip on Taffy's bridle. "I want to make sure Taffy hasn't taken a general dislike to her saddle before I hand over the reins. We wouldn't want a repeat of today's adventure, would we?"

"I reckon not," Andi said with a sigh. She gave in and let Mitch coddle her a minute more. When he seemed satisfied the mare had put her earlier scare behind her, he handed Andi the reins and mounted Chase.

"Now we can go," he said.

Mitch took his time. His pace forced Andi to keep Taffy at a leisurely lope, broken up with long periods of walking. At this rate, it would be close to sundown before they arrived home. Her stomach rumbled. *I hope Mother holds supper for us.* She giggled.

"What's so funny?" Mitch asked.

"I told Lucy I'd beat her home, but I didn't." Andi lost her smile. "She asked me to ride home with her. If I had, none of this would have happened."

"True," Mitch agreed. "But that tack might have stayed lodged in your gear and gone unnoticed until the next time you saddled Taffy . . ." He left the rest unsaid. "God works things out for our good," he reminded her. "Don't dwell on what-ifs."

Andi nodded. "You're right. If I rode home with Lucy, Macy and I would still be enemies. So it did turn out better this way."

By the time they trotted into the yard, Andi felt nearly back to normal. The ride around town had helped sort out her feelings about Macy. Better still, Mitch's quiet approval on the way home went a long way in assuring Andi that she had for once done the right thing.

"I'm proud of you, Sis," Mitch said when he halted Chase next to the barn. He dismounted and offered Andi a hand down. She took it. "I had a bad feeling when you hightailed it back to town. I expected to see my sister disgracing herself and our family name by fighting like a no-account Hollister in the middle of the street. I was pleasantly surprised when I caught up and saw what was going on. You reined in your temper mighty fine today."

Andi flushed at the praise and ducked her head. "I felt so sorry for Macy that I didn't feel angry anymore. Only sad."

"Go inside and wash up for supper," Mitch said. "I'll tend your horse."

"Where have you two been?" Chad called from the dim interior of the barn. He strode outside and into the twilight of the yard. "Did you get those supplies I sent you for?"

Mitch untied a heavy sack from behind his saddle. "Yep." He gave it a toss.

Chad caught the sack and laid it aside. "What about the telegram I asked you to send?"

"All wired and safely on its way."

"What took you so long?"

"I had some family business to attend to." Mitch exchanged a knowing glance with Andi, who stood beside Taffy, listening to every word.

Chad looked at her. "What kind of trouble are you in now?"

Andi bristled, but Mitch jumped in too fast to give her time to argue. "Well, aside from the fact that our little sister was almost killed when Taffy ran away—"

"Taffy a runaway?" Chad cut in. He shook his head. "Not possible."

"If a tack were lodged under Sky's saddle, he'd be a runaway too," Andi said. "Show him, Mitch."

Mitch fished the wicked-looking piece of metal from his vest pocket and dropped it into Chad's gloved hand. "There you go. Chase and I caught up and saved the day, but that's a ride I never want to make again. I don't know what would have happened if I hadn't seen Taffy flash by."

Frowning, Chad fingered the tack. "Sorry for snapping at you, Sis. Lucky thing Mitch was in town." He handed the tack to Andi. "Who would do this to you?"

"Macy Walker. I got her into trouble today at school. This was her payback." Andi slipped the tack into her pocket to throw away later.

"The girl was being egged on by one of the Walkers," Mitch added. "He was trying to get them to fight." He scowled in disgust. "No good's going to come from *any* of that bunch if you ask me."

"Walker . . . Walker . . ." Chad rubbed the back of his neck, trying to place the name.

"You've seen them," Mitch said. "One or two are always loafing around town. Sheriff says they're a nuisance, but no more so than the rest of the riffraff in the warehouse district. They come, they stay awhile, they cause trouble, and then they either leave town or are run out."

He pulled Andi into a quick hug. "If Macy is their sister, she's got it rough putting up with those roughnecks."

"Her brothers are scary," Andi told Chad. "They treat Macy real mean. I hope Sheriff Tate arrests them all."

"I'll let Russ manage his town," Chad said. "We have more important things to occupy our time than worrying about Fresno's rowdies."

Andi sighed. Of course they did. She turned to go.

"What's the bad news?" Mitch asked.

"Four more steers and a couple of calves went missing from the southwest range. Sid swears he didn't hear or see anything suspicious. These rustlers are like phantoms. They strike, make off with a few head, and vanish. They never hit the same area twice. Worse . . ." His voice dropped, and Andi paused just beyond the barn to listen. "Brett McLaughlin told me this afternoon that he's lost three yearling colts."

"*Colts?*" Andi ran back to Chad. "They're cattle rustlers. They don't steal horses."

Mitch whistled. "Sounds like they're bound and determined to get themselves invited to a necktie party."

"If *I* catch up with whoever's behind this, they won't need a rope for the hanging." Chad started for the house. "You coming, Mitch? Andi? Mother held supper on account of Miss Hawkins joining us. I might even let Justin off from night duty this evening so he can escort his beloved back to town."

"Generous of you," Andi said, too low for Chad to hear. He was already halfway to the house.

Mitch chuckled and took hold of Taffy's reins. "Go on, Sis. I said I'd put up your horse."

"Thanks." She followed Chad across the yard and plucked his sleeve. "Chad?" Her heart fluttered. Rustling had suddenly turned personal. "Are my colts safe?"

Chad stopped. "Don't worry, little sister." His voice turned soft. "The twins are safe as they can be, I promise. They're in the near paddock. Besides, McLaughlin's spread is miles away. The rustlers won't come here." He reached out to ruffle Andi's hair, but she ducked.

"I'm almost fourteen years old," she said, laughing. "Much too old for you to muss my hair."

"Oh, yeah?" Chad snatched at her.

Andi dodged her brother and went squealing up the porch steps and into the house.

⸺

First thing Monday morning, Sam Blake met Andi in front of his livery. It was obvious he'd been on the lookout for her. He reached for Taffy's bridle and started right in. "Miss Andi, I can't tell you how sorry I am about last Friday. I always check your saddle." He shook his head. "My place's got a good reputation. To think that somebody could sneak in and—"

"It's not your fault, Mr. Blake," Andi assured him as she dismounted. "I'm fine, Taffy's fine, so let's forget it."

"If you say so." He still sounded annoyed for letting something like this get past him.

Cory appeared, books and lunch pail in hand. "So long, Pa. Come on, Andi. I'll walk you to school." He seemed in a hurry to get Andi alone.

"What's wrong?" she asked when they'd gone half a block.

Cory's blue-gray eyes held remorse. "I saw what happened on Friday, and I heard the story how Mitch barely rescued you in time—"

"News sure travels fast in this town."

"Yeah," Cory agreed. "I just want to say"—he swallowed—"I'm sorry I talked you into standing up to Macy. You might have been killed, and it would've been my fault."

Andi was touched by Cory's concern, but it wasn't his fault. It was Macy's. "It's over, Cory. Stop fretting. Besides, God worked it out. Macy and I are friends now."

Cory snorted. "Friends? I wouldn't trust her." He shifted his tin pail and reached out a hand. "You've had a bad time. Let me carry your books."

"We only have a block to go." But Cory gave her such a pleading look that Andi relented. "Sure. Why not?" She plunked her books into his arms and wondered why boys were so silly. She was perfectly capable of carrying her own books to school.

Andi slid into the double seat a few minutes later with sudden misgivings about her new friend. Cory's warning rang in her ears: *I wouldn't trust her.* Maybe he was right. After spending the weekend with her brothers, Macy might change her mind about wanting to see the colts or be friends. *If that happens, I'm through*, Andi decided. If Mr. Foster refused to move her to a new seat, she would ask her mother to intervene.

Mitch had told the runaway story around the supper table last Friday to a rapt audience. Mother listened quietly then said, "All's well that ends well." But her face paled during the retelling. After what happened, it was unlikely the teacher would stand up to Elizabeth Carter if she insisted Andi have a new seat.

Andi was pleasantly surprised—and more than a little relieved—when Macy plunked down next to her and slapped the primer on the desktop. "I ain't sayin' it'll do any good, but I'll try it a day or two." She gave Andi a crooked smile. "I still wanna see them colts too."

"I'll ask Mr. Foster if I can help you after I finish my lessons. We can also study before and after school."

Macy opened the book to the first page. "I know most o' the letters, but they look all a jumble when they're squished together."

Andi flipped through the primer until she found a page of simple words. "Let's start here." She scooted closer. "Each letter makes a sound. When you put the sounds together, the letters spell words." Sitting next to Macy, Andi wondered if her new friend had taken time over the weekend to bathe. She didn't stink near as much as she had last week.

Then again, Andi mused, *maybe I'm just not noticing it.*

CHAPTER 16

Mother says if I could walk a mile in another person's shoes, I would learn why they act like they do. If Macy had shoes, I would walk in them for a mile and find out why she stays with her worthless brothers.

It astonished Andi how fast Macy caught on to reading. On Monday she learned to read simple words like *cat*, *rat*, and *fat*. By Friday afternoon, she had finished the entire primer.

The girls were sitting on a bench outside the millinery shop when Macy closed the book and dropped it in Andi's lap. "You can have this one back and bring me another," she announced. "Readin' ain't so hard."

Andi gave her a puzzled look. Underneath her coarse exterior, Macy hid a quick mind. "You could have learned to read ages ago. Why didn't you?"

Macy smirked. "Reckon I was too busy causin' a ruckus to care. Never stayed long enough in one place neither. And nobody ever took the time to . . ." She cleared her throat. "It don't matter. I read good now. Pretty soon I'll read better than the boys."

"That shouldn't be too hard," Andi said. A vision of the uncouth, wild-haired brother from last Friday came and went.

Macy hooted. "Yep. My brothers ain't educated or ree-fined. They got worse manners than a weasel in a henhouse." She stretched her legs out on the wooden sidewalk and wiggled her bare toes. "My manners ain't any better. We're ornery cusses."

"You've got three brothers, right?" Andi said.

Macy scowled. "Yeah. You saw Ty the day he brung me t' class. He's the oldest, so he thinks he can thrash me when he likes. But I ain't scared of him. Then there's Jase and Rudy."

Macy grew quiet. "Jase an' me ignore each other. Rudy's the scary one. He's got a mean mouth, a hair trigger, and a heavy hand." She shivered. "I try t' stay outta his way."

Andi could understand that. "So where do you *really* live? You can't hang around the saloons all the time. Or sleep in sheds."

"Ty says we'll settle down someday with all kinds o' livestock. Maybe even chickens. But right now they're holing up in the foothills—some dark, gloomy canyon. I seen it once. I don't like it." She shuddered. "I stay in town but I 'spect Ty'll drag me out there sooner or later. He don't like leavin' me on my own."

"What do they do out there? Hunt? Keep cattle?"

"I don't know and I don't care." Macy kicked at a loose board in the walk. "My brothers ain't what you call hard workin'. They spend most o' their time drinkin', fightin', and causin' trouble." She shrugged. "Enough about *my* kin. What about you? You got any family besides that one brother?"

Andi nodded. "We have a ranch about an hour's ride east of town. I've got three brothers and two sisters. My oldest sister lives in San Francisco. My father's dead, but I've got the world's best mother."

"What happened to your pa?"

"He was killed when his horse threw him during roundup one year. I was little and don't remember it much. I do remember crying and not understanding why Father wasn't there anymore. My brother Justin knew just what to say and do to help me get over it." She smiled at Macy. "Big brothers are nice to have around."

Macy made a face. "No, they ain't. They're downright mean and bigger than me. I wish I could—" She clamped her jaw shut and stared at her lap.

Does she wish she could get away from them? Andi wondered. *I know I would.* "What about your folks? Where are they?"

"Pa died a few years after the War, just afore I was born. You Yankees left a bullet in his back that slowly killed him." She sniffed. "Soon as Ma birthed me, she took off with a travelin' gambler. Reckon she didn't wanna be tied down with four young'uns and no man around."

"I'm sorry," Andi said softly.

"Ain't your fault." She let out a long, lonely sigh. "I sure do miss havin' a ma, though. Bet she wouldn't let them older ones boss me."

Andi gave Macy a knowing grin. "Mine boss me too. That's how it is when you're the youngest—mother or no mother."

Macy perked up a little. "Reckon so."

"Do you have any other relatives?"

"I got kin back in Arkansas, around Fayetteville. Pa's sister Hester took us in when Ma left." Macy's eyes brightened. "I liked it there. Aunt Hester was good t' me. But Ty hated her. Said she was fillin' our heads with fool notions about a God who looks out for folks. I'd just turned eight when Ty yanked us all outta there."

"You've been wandering homeless ever since?"

Macy nodded. Her eyes were red but no tears leaked out. "Aunt Hester tried to keep me with her, but Ty said no. He didn't want our Bible-thumpin' aunt turnin' me into a goody-goody. 'Ain't nobody gonna look after you better than us, Macy-girl,' Ty told me. He says that all the time." She paused. "Aunt Hester did a lot of cryin' when we left. I ain't seen the home folks since."

Andi sat lost in thought. At Macy's bleak recital, gratitude for her own family welled up. Her birthday celebration last Sunday after church had resonated with laughter, gifts, and good food. Later that evening Justin had put his arm around Lucy and announced their July wedding date. Stuffed full of *tamales* and birthday cake, Andi cheered along with the rest of her family.

"When can I see your colts?"

Macy's words startled Andi, bringing her back to the present. "Anytime you want to ride out."

"Ain't got no horse, and your place sounds too far to walk barefoot. Or even with boots if I had any."

Andi looked down at Macy's rough, bare feet. They were caked with dirt and scratched by brambles and rocks. She felt ashamed. At home she must have a dozen different pairs of shoes, boots, and slippers. "Listen, Macy," she said. "If you're not too proud to take them, I've an extra pair of shoes at home. They're too tight for me, but your feet might be smaller. Would you like them?"

"Your ma wouldn't care?"

"Not at all." An idea took shape. "Come out to the ranch with me. I'll give you the shoes and you can see the colts."

Macy sucked in her breath. "You mean it? Right now? Me?"

Andi laughed. "Of course *you*. We can ride double on Taffy."

Macy shot to her feet and yanked Andi up with her. "Let's go before you change your mind."

Andi was about to tell Macy she had no intention of changing her mind, when a dark shadow fell over them. She whirled and saw a tall man with a rough-shaven face and dark hair that hung to his shoulders. He was glowering at Macy.

Swell. Another ornery brother, Andi thought. *They sure do show up at the worst times.*

Macy took one look at the man and scowled. "What d'ya want, Jase? I'm in a hurry."

He grabbed Macy's arm. "Ty wants you out at the canyon for the next few days. Him and me got business up Madera way. You're gonna help Rudy keep an eye on things while we're gone."

"No, I ain't. I hate that place." Macy gave Andi a troubled look. "You better go."

Jase ran his dark gaze over Andi. "Get outta here," he snarled.

Andi took off down the street, only too anxious to leave. She felt Jase

Walker's eyes on her until she turned the corner. Even then, she didn't feel safe until she ducked into Blake's livery. Fingers shaking, she started saddling her horse.

"I can do that," Cory offered, stepping into the aisle. He set aside the pitchfork he was using and walked over. "I'm working for Pa this afternoon."

Andi shook her head. "I'm fine."

Before Cory could argue, a loud, insistent voice filled the livery. "I need a horse!" Macy stomped in and slapped the rent money into Cory's palm. He gaped at her and didn't move. Macy raised a fist. "Ain't my money good enough? Hurry up or else."

While Cory scrambled to find a horse, Macy joined Andi. "I told Jase you was just a girl I met. And that I didn't know your name."

"Why?" Andi tightened the cinch and let the stirrup fall into place.

"I don't want him to know I got a friend." She glanced around to make sure Cory was out of earshot. "Back in Arkansas I knew a boy. Deke was just my age. We had fun 'til"—Macy clenched her jaw—"'til Rudy beat him up. Deke was from the 'wrong' clan."

Andi swallowed. Macy had indeed done her a favor. She didn't want the Walker brothers to know who she was. She grabbed the reins and led Taffy out into the afternoon sun. Macy followed.

"Do you have to go out to the canyon?" Andi asked.

Macy nodded glumly. "I'll feel Ty's belt if I don't."

"When will I see you again?"

"Don't rightly know. Jase just told me to rent a horse and get out there." She scuffed a bare toe at the dirt. "I don't know what the boys are up to. Most likely some scheme that'll get us all hung."

Andi gasped. *"What?"*

Macy laughed and looked away. "Just funnin' ya. I'm riled at Jase is all. Don't pay me no mind."

Andi had no chance to answer. Cory walked up leading a small, black horse saddled and bridled. His expression said it all: *You better take good care of this horse.*

Macy glared at Cory until he dropped the reins into her hands and went back to work. Then she mounted up. "G'bye, Andi." Without waiting for a reply, she touched the black's sides and trotted away.

Andi watched her go. A tiny shiver crept up her neck. What kind of trouble was Macy riding into?

CHAPTER 17

Macy could be a good friend if she wasn't so unpredictable. It wears me out wondering what she'll say or do next.

Wednesday morning Macy plunked into the seat beside Andi with a loud *thump.* "You got them shoes?" she demanded. "And the next reader?" Without waiting for an answer, she leaned her arms on her desk and dropped her head down. She looked bone-tired.

"Howdy to you too," Andi replied, stung. "You sure know how to tear into folks."

Macy raised her dirt-streaked face. "Too bad. I been workin' like a dog and I'm done in. Do you got 'em or not?"

Andi wanted to snap at Macy to go find her own reader, but the red welt across the girl's cheek brought her up short. "Yes, I kept them at school," she said. "I didn't know when you'd get back from the canyon."

Macy groaned and hid her face in her arms.

"What's wrong?"

"Nothin'."

Andi leaned over and whispered close to Macy's ear. "Your shoes are in the cloakroom. You can try them on after school. Here's your *First Reader.*" She shoved the book next to Macy's hand.

Andi waited for Macy's response. She wanted to see her friend's eyes sparkle when she opened the book and discovered she could read the harder text. Macy would probably bury herself in the book and not come up until noon recess. Andi expected a dozen nudges this morning when she couldn't figure out a word.

But Macy didn't react. She didn't touch the reader. Andi frowned. *She could at least say thank you.*

The book lay untouched next to Macy's slumped form all morning. Her soft snoring showed she'd been lulled to sleep by the warm classroom and the schoolmaster's droning voice. Toward noontime, she snuffled and turned her head. Asleep, Macy looked young and vulnerable. A dark bruise stood out under the welt. *Did she fall? Or did somebody hit her?* Andi did not want to guess.

Macy slept through the noon recess and the afternoon session. Nobody woke her. When a few boys snickered at her snores, Mr. Foster silenced them with a dark look.

At four o'clock the schoolmaster dismissed class. Macy slept on. Andi finally shook her shoulder. "Wake up. School's out."

Macy jerked awake. She wiped the drool from her mouth and sat up blinking. "Huh? What?"

"You slept through the whole day and got away with it." Andi didn't know why. A swift reprimand always fell on a dozing student. Mr. Foster either felt rare compassion for his rowdy student or he wanted to avoid disrupting his class so close to school's end. "Let's go."

Macy yawned and stretched then followed Andi to the cloakroom. She plopped down and slipped the high-topped shoes over her bare feet. A row of tiny, unfastened buttons climbed one side of each shoe. Macy looked stumped.

Andi squatted beside her and held up a buttonhook. "This will help." She let Macy fumble with one button before finishing the job for her. It took time and practice to deal with the pesky buttons. Andi preferred riding boots that slipped on.

"Let's ride out to the ranch," Andi offered when she saw how mismatched Macy looked. "I'll find some stockings to go with your shoes, and a dress too. Then we can see the colts."

Macy whooped, wide awake at last. "Let's find your horse and get outta town before another brother comes lookin' for me." She shot down the classroom stairs. "You comin'?" she hollered over her shoulder.

Macy chattered like a magpie all the way out to the ranch. She also read aloud from her new *First Reader*. Every few minutes she prodded Andi to help her with the hard words. By the time they trotted into the yard, Andi's ears were ringing. "Here we are." She waved to a couple of ranch hands and slid from Taffy's back.

"You live *here*?" Macy's gaze flitted from the Spanish-style *hacienda* with its dazzling white stucco walls and red-tiled roof to the enormous red barn and freshly painted outbuildings. She dismounted, pocketed the book, and turned a circle to see it all. "You're rich," she whispered.

Andi didn't say anything. She took hold of Taffy's reins and led her into the barn. Macy stumbled after her, eyes wide. She looked overwhelmed and out of place.

Hoping to make Macy feel at home, Andi tossed her a brush. "Want to help?"

Macy caught the brush and nervously began grooming the golden palomino. Soon, however, her smile returned. So did her chatter. Andi smiled back. There was nothing like grooming a horse to settle a ruffled spirit.

"What I wouldn't give to have me a place like this," Macy said with a heartfelt sigh.

"Maybe someday you can. Didn't Ty say—?"

"Ty lies a lot," Macy muttered. She drew her brows together and turned away. Her brush sailed along Taffy's rump. "We ain't never gonna settle dow—" Macy sucked in a sharp breath and let out a cry. She staggered backward.

Andi dropped her brush and rushed over. "What's wrong? You look like you've seen a ghost."

"N-nothin's wrong." Macy wagged her head. "I . . . I just feel wore out all of a sudden."

"I'm sorry, Macy. I forgot your brothers made you work so hard. We can finish this later. Let's go inside."

Macy shook her head. "I'm fine now." She ran her hand along Taffy's rump. "Uh . . . whose brand is this?"

"It's ours. The Circle C, for Carter." She waved at Macy to follow her out of the barn. "Come on."

"Your family's the richest in the valley!" Macy stood gaping.

Andi rolled her eyes. "Yes, I've heard that. So what?"

"I gotta go. I can't be here." She looked ready to flee.

"Why not?" Andi's heart sank. What did Macy know about the Carter family that she didn't like? Had Mitch had another run-in with Rudy? "Don't you want to see the colts?"

Macy's face scrunched up. She seemed torn between staying and leaving. "Yeah . . ." She pressed her lips together and said no more. Something was troubling Macy, but she didn't look ready to share what it was.

Andi let out a disappointed breath. "I'll take you back to town if you like, but I have a surprise if you stay."

"A surprise?" Color returned to Macy's cheeks. She glanced at Taffy and shrugged. "I reckon it can't hurt."

Andi led Macy out of the barn, through the kitchen entrance, and up the back stairs. "This way to the surprise," she said with a grin.

Curiosity wiped the troubled look from Macy's face. "What is it?" she asked eagerly.

Andi laughed. "If I told you, then it wouldn't be a surprise." She threw open the door to the washroom, where a porcelain bathtub stood on brass feet.

Macy gasped. "A bathing room—right inside the house!"

"Yep." Andi sprinkled a handful of soap powder into the tub and grabbed a bucket. "But we have to haul the hot water," she said.

Macy couldn't help Andi fast enough. As soon as the last bucketful splashed into the tub, Macy stripped and crawled in. Water and bubbles rose clear to the edges, nearly spilling over. She lay back, eyes closed. Only her face showed. "Ain't never had a bubble bath before." She raised a hand and blew the suds away. "A dip in the creek don't hold a candle to this." She ducked under the water and came up soaping her matted, dirty hair.

Water splashed out of the tub. Andi jumped back, lifting a blue calico dress out of danger. "Bubble baths are a lot of fun," she agreed. "What about this? Do you like it?"

Macy squinted through the soap bubbles. "*Like* it?" She rubbed her eyes. "I can't borrow a dress like that. I might rip it or somethin'."

"You can have it." Andi smiled. Whatever had bothered Macy earlier seemed to have passed. "Mother told me last week to go through my things and sort out the old ones from last summer. We're giving them to the orphanage. You might as well take a couple for yourself." She laid the dress aside.

Andi turned back just in time to see Macy bend over and plunge her face in the water. Dark-red lines crisscrossed her back and shoulders. A bruise inched its way around the base of her neck. Amidst the bubbles, other bruises dotted the backs of her arms. Andi stepped back in alarm. Her feet slid out from under her, and she crashed to the floor, breathing hard.

Macy grabbed a towel and shot up from the tub. "What happened?" She wrapped the towel around herself and shook the water from her hair. "You all right?"

Andi licked her dry lips and stared at Macy. *No, I am not all right.*

Macy spoke freely about being thrashed, but Andi had no idea what that really meant until today. For all Chad's threatening to tan her hide when she annoyed him, he'd never touched her. Not once. Neither had anyone else—not like this. The few well-deserved swats Mother had applied to her backside when she was little didn't compare. Not by a long shot.

A chill ran down Andi's spine. She closed her eyes while Macy pulled on under drawers, a stiff petticoat, and the blue and white dress. Andi couldn't watch. She didn't want to see any more marks.

When Andi opened her eyes, Macy was regarding her with a look that showed she knew. Water dripped from her hair and ran down her dress. She crouched beside Andi. "Ain't never seen myself from behind. Is it that bad?" When Andi nodded, she shrugged. "Don't pay it no mind. I don't."

"You should!" Andi scrambled to her feet and found a chair. She grasped Macy's hands. "Why don't you run away? Leave those rotten brothers. You could—"

Macy's high-pitched laugh silenced Andi. "You're crazy. Where would I go? Ty would find me and haul me back." She dropped her gaze. "Kinfolk stick together."

"What about Aunt Hester?" Andi asked. "She's your kin."

A faraway look came to Macy's eyes. Then she blinked. "It's been too long. She don't want me back. Besides, I ain't got no money. Don't know how to get back there neither." Her face turned hard. "I ain't leavin'. They're all I got. We're family."

Some family, Andi thought, but she held her angry retort inside. Macy clearly didn't want to talk about it. To keep her mind off what she'd seen, Andi picked up a brush and ran it through her friend's pale, shoulder-length tangles. A snip here and there from a pair of shears evened everything out. "There. You look nice." She handed Macy a hand mirror.

A soft intake of breath told Andi that Macy agreed.

"It's hard to imagine you ever punched Cory or did all those mean things at school," Andi said. "I think . . ." She paused.

"What?"

"I think that deep down you just want to be an ordinary girl like the rest of us. But living with those rough brothers never gave you a chance to learn how."

Macy nodded. Tears filled her eyes, and this time she didn't try to hide them or brush them away. "Ain't nobody *ever* been as nice to me as you," she said. "Ain't nobody tried so hard to be my friend neither. Why would you—a respectable girl from a rich family—bother with the likes of me? 'Specially when I've been so mean and spiteful."

A dozen reasons came to Andi's mind: *My sister nagged me. I promised Mr. Foster. It's the Christian thing to do. My mother expects it. I didn't want to be expelled for punching you* . . .

Andi tossed those shallow answers aside. Only one reason mattered—the real one. "It's because I decided to care."

Macy's eyes and nose ran freely. "I'm glad." She lifted the hem of her dress and brought it up to her face.

"Macy, no!" Andi hollered, aghast. She whipped out her bandana and shoved it in Macy's hands. Then she broke into uncontrollable giggles. "I think you've got a lot to learn."

Macy rolled her eyes and blew her nose. "I reckon you're right." She tied the used bandana around her neck. "Can we go see them colts now?"

CHAPTER 18

There's something special about horses. They bring folks together. I never would have dreamed that Macy loves horses as much as I do.

Shasta and Sunny galloped up to the fence at Andi's first whistle. They nuzzled her and whinnied, imploring her to come in and play. The yearlings joined the twins at the railing. They jostled each other in their attempts to get attention.

"Come on, Macy," Andi urged as she climbed the fence. "Let's go in and play with them."

"We can do that?"

"Why not? They're mine."

"What about them other colts?"

Andi jumped down into the large field. "Most are headed to the yearling sale next month. The more we handle them, the happier the buyers will be. They won't hurt you." She slapped the neck of a large paint horse. "Go on, Apache. I'm not here to give you all the attention. You get enough already."

Macy stood transfixed, staring at the two dozen young horses. "These are the prettiest horses I ever saw," she said in a hushed voice. "How do you choose the ones you like best?"

Andi paused and considered. She was so used to seeing the young stock she hardly noticed how they might appear to an outsider. Shiny bays, three coal-black fillies, a few paint horses, sorrels of all shades, a palomino, and her own creamy Sunny and chocolate palomino, Shasta, made up the herd. A rainbow of horse colors. *Gorgeous!* Ripples of delight made her heart leap. "I can't choose. I love them all."

Just then Sunny trotted up behind Macy. He gave her a playful nudge, which sent her sprawling to the ground. She yelped.

"Sunny!" Andi rebuked her colt. "For shame. Where are your manners?"

Macy leaped to her feet and brushed the loose grass from her dress. Her eyes glittered. "Don't scold him. He didn't hurt me none." She reached out a tentative hand. "I think he likes me." Sunny snorted and stepped forward so Macy could rub his nose.

"He likes to be scratched just under his forelock," Andi said. "He'll stand there for as long as you want to bother with him."

Macy immediately put Andi's words to the test. She rubbed and scratched, and the little colt stood still as a statue. Macy rested her head against his neck and kept at it.

"I told you," Andi said. "Sunny is spoiled rotten. He and Shasta are weanlings but they think they're yearlings." She laughed. "You can stand there and pamper him some more, or we can make them run."

"Let's make 'em run!"

An hour later, Andi knew Macy had fallen in love with Sunny. The cream colt appeared taken with Macy as well, which was astonishing. Sunny was the skittish and capricious twin. Many days Andi exhausted herself with his training; on other days he behaved beautifully. Chad sometimes wanted to smack Sunny's hard head. He didn't, but Andi could feel his frustration. The colt had a mind of his own and a temperament she couldn't figure out.

Until this afternoon, no one could have convinced Andi that Sunny would endear himself to a perfect stranger. He had never acted like a docile lamb around anyone except Andi. Now he followed Macy around the field, nuzzling her to lead him and handle him as if they'd known each other since his foaling.

"It's the most peculiar thing I ever saw," Andi confessed when the small band of horses followed them across the paddock. "None of the hands trust Sunny. He's pretty and he's smart, but he's also . . . well . . . kind of flighty. Our foreman, Sid, swears Sunny got a taste of locoweed when he was little." She frowned. "That's not true, of course. He'd have to have a steady diet of it to be affected."

"Kinda flighty?" Macy scowled. "He ain't nothin' of the kind. He's perfect. I . . . I love him," she said fiercely, as if she dared Andi to deny it. She engulfed the colt in a tight hug and buried her face in his white mane. Sunny nickered softly.

"I can see that," Andi replied with a smile. "Love at first sight, the both of you," she teased. "I love him too, and Shasta. I can sit for hours just watching them gallop, with their manes flying and their tails stretched out. But . . ." Her voice trailed off when the two of them reached the fence.

"But what?"

Andi leaned against the white railings. "Chad says I'll have to sell them eventually. 'This is a working ranch,'" she quoted, deepening her voice to sound like Chad's. "'We raise stock to sell, not to keep as pets.'"

Macy caught her breath. "Would you sell them as yearlings?"

"No. I'll wait until they're three-year-olds. Chad says by then I'll be so sick of all the work that goes into them that I'll be glad to see them go." She grinned. "Besides, Taffy will most likely have another foal by then to take most of my attention."

"How much would a horse like Sunny cost?" Macy asked.

Andi bit her lip. She didn't want to discourage her new friend with the cold, hard facts. Circle C horses were some of the finest horses in the state. "Oh, quite a bit," she replied vaguely.

Macy sighed. "I could never hope to own a horse like Sunny." Then she smiled. "But it's a fine thing just to be able to play with him."

"I'm glad you're having fun. I didn't know you liked horses."

"Neither did I," Macy said with a laugh. Her whole face lit up with what looked like a new inner joy. "This is the first time I've ever really been around horses. Aunt Hester had an old swayback I used to ride, but I don't know if he rightly counts as a horse. Useless ol' nag." She started scratching Sunny again. "He wasn't nothin' like these beauties."

"Andi!" A loud call from across the yard broke into the girls' conversation. Chad strolled over to the fence and leaned over the railing. He shoved his hat back off his forehead. "Who's your friend?"

"This is Macy." She turned to Macy. "This is my brother Chad."

"Howdy," Macy chirped.

Chad gave her a quick nod. "Howdy." He looked at Andi, eyebrows raised. His unspoken question hung in the air. *This the same Macy who nearly killed you?*

Andi nodded.

Chad grunted and turned back to the horses. "How are the twins coming along?"

"Fine," Andi answered. "We were playing today. I wanted to show them off to Macy. I'll do some real work with them tomorrow after school."

"I see. Well, you best get washed up for supper."

"Is it that late already?" Andi shaded her eyes and glanced west. The sun was still well above the horizon. "I have to take Macy back to town."

"There's no time. I have to eat and get out to the herd before long. Got an idea the rustlers are going to try something out toward the river tonight."

Andi didn't answer. So far, none of Sid's or Chad's or the other ranchers' "ideas" had brought them any closer to catching the cattle thieves. The rustlers were probably holed up somewhere snug as you please and having a good laugh over how they managed to stay one step ahead of the stockmen. There was no sign they were butchering the beef and carting it off. They must be changing the brands and selling the cattle. But where?

Rush, rush, rush, Andi griped silently. She'd forgotten supper was being served earlier these days, ever since rustling had taken over her brothers' lives. "I reckon I'll miss supper then," she said. "Come on, Macy. I'll take you back."

"Mother won't be happy," Chad warned. "I'll ask Rosa to set an extra plate at the table for your friend." Without waiting for a reply, he dogtrotted back to the house.

Rush, rush, rush. "We better wash up," Andi said.

Macy looked sick. "I dunno. Ain't never ate with fancy folks before."

"The food's good if you can stand the conversation," she said. "Come on."

Five minutes into the meal Andi wished Lucy had surprised Justin and shown up for supper. Melinda and Lucy usually chatted about wedding plans. Andi would have welcomed their talk tonight. Her guest looked out of place. She sat hunched in her chair and timidly picked at her food.

"What I can't figure out," Chad was saying, "is where they're keeping the cattle. Phil Jenkins thinks it's up in the foothills, but"—he shook his head—"that's an awful lot of ground to cover."

"How many cows has the Bent Pine lost?" Justin wanted to know.

Andi dug her spoon into her steaming stew and frowned. *If Lucy was here, you would not ask that question.*

"A dozen," came Chad's reply. "They're not as easy to steal as ours. But those missing beeves hurt Phil more than the hundred we've lost so far. The Bent Pine isn't a big spread. Phil needs every head he's got. He's running scared, and I don't blame him. McLaughlin is thinking about hiring more men to spot the cattle, but I doubt it'll do much good." Chad shook his head. "How do you cover that much rangeland, especially at night?"

Nobody answered.

Andi felt sorry for Macy. Any other time, a guest at the Carter table was treated like royalty. When Lucy had joined them the other night, Justin made sure rustling news was kept to a minimum. Why didn't he do that tonight? *I reckon Macy doesn't count as a guest,* she decided.

Her family was polite but distant. Maybe nobody could forget what Macy had done to Andi a week and a half ago. She quickly squelched that idea. Mother, especially, did not hold grudges. Andi let out a quiet breath. Macy hadn't said one word during supper. It was time she returned to town.

Andi glanced out the dining room window. There was no chance Mother would let her take Macy back, not with the sun setting so quickly. "Macy needs a ride to town," she announced during a lull in the conversation.

"Sorry, can't help you," Chad said. His reluctance to give up one of his men felt like a slap to Andi.

"Justin tied Thunder to the buggy and drove Lucy back to town the other night," she protested. "Why can't somebody do the same for Macy? All you ever talk about is cows and rustling. And you're prickly as cactus lately."

"Well, little sister," Chad retorted, "you'd be prickly too if you were on guard duty day and night, along with all your other responsibilities. You should try it sometime."

"How about tonight?" Andi snapped, perfectly serious.

"Andrea, that will do," her mother said sharply.

Andi fell silent.

"Perhaps Macy can stay the night," Mother suggested. "You girls can ride to school in the morning. That way Chad needn't give up one of his guards." She turned to Macy with a warm smile. "As long as your folks won't worry."

"My folks?" Macy squeaked. She stared at her bowl of half-eaten stew. "I don't wanna be a bother, ma'am."

"You're no bother," Mother assured her.

"That's right, Macy," Andi said. "It's more of a bother for Chad to take you back to town. May we be excused, Mother? I'm tired of cattle-rustling talk." She shot Chad a sour look.

When Mother gave her permission, Andi pushed back her chair. "Come on, Macy. Let's run out and see the colts one more time before it gets pitch dark."

Macy shrugged. "Sure." She gave Andi an unenthusiastic smile and shuffled behind her to the paddock.

"What's wrong?" Andi asked as they watched the sun go down in a blaze of orange and red.

Macy's gaze was fixed on the road that led to town. She sighed. "Nothin'. Nothin' at all."

CHAPTER 19

Sneaking around in the middle of the night is a really dumb idea.

Andi gasped and sat up in bed, heart pounding. Sweat beaded her forehead. *What a horrible dream!* Fear clutched her throat. *Shasta and Sunny . . . gone!* She shivered, pulled her legs up, and wrapped her arms around her knees. "I just had a dream that scared me silly," she whispered to the lump sleeping next to her. "Rustlers made off with my colts and I never saw them again." Her eyes smarted with unshed tears. "It was so real."

The lump didn't answer.

"Macy?" A half-moon peeked through the glass balcony doors, casting a pale, silvery light into the room. The bundle of blankets beside her lay motionless. "Hey, wake up." She reached out to shake what she thought was Macy's shoulder, but her hand felt only softness. "What in the world?"

Andi snatched the covers and yanked them aside. No Macy. Instead, a pile of pillows marked the place where her friend had curled up only a short while ago. Andi reached a hand under the pillows. The spot was still warm. "Macy?" She turned up the lamp on her night table. Light spilled into the room, making her blink. "Are you here?"

No answer. Perhaps she'd gone to the washroom.

Andi left her bed and tiptoed down the hall. The washroom stood dark and empty. Chewing on her lip, she returned to her room stumped. Had her new friend gone downstairs for a midnight snack without asking? She might not know about guest etiquette. Macy had compared her manners to that of a weasel. *Does a weasel ask permission to snatch a bite to eat from the henhouse?*

Andi bit back a chuckle at the analogy. The remnants of her nightmare faded, replaced by uneasiness at Macy's disappearance. She stuffed her bare feet into her riding boots and pulled a lounging robe over her white cotton nightgown. Tossing her hair out of her face, she headed for the narrow steps that led down to the kitchen. She couldn't go back to sleep until she found Macy.

Andi hurried down the back stairs and paused to listen. All was quiet except for the faint ticking coming from the grandfather clock in the hallway. She cracked the stairwell door open and peeked into the kitchen. Moonlight glimmered through the windows. It gave enough light for Andi to pass through without banging into the cookstove or tripping over the cat. She sighed, disappointed. The kitchen was deserted.

She opened the back door and glanced around outside. A soft thumping sound drew her attention to the barn. Her breath caught. "Macy?" A small, dark shadow darted from tree to tree, avoiding the moonlight. Andi watched the figure disappear into the barn.

"It's got to be Macy." Andi closed the kitchen door and tiptoed down the porch steps. Then she cut across the yard toward the barn. A sudden *clunk* and the sound of footsteps sent Andi ducking behind a tree, just like the shadowy figure she was following had done.

When Andi reached the barn, she slipped through the narrow opening between the double doors. "Macy?" she called. Her voice cracked. "Are you in here?" She crept down the aisle then yelped when she tripped over a bucket. It clattered like a gunshot in the still night.

From behind, a hand clamped over Andi's mouth. She took a breath to scream, but a voice in her ear hissed, "Shhh." The hand fell away.

Andi spun around, spitting mad. "What got into you, scaring me like that?" she demanded. "And why are you in our barn?"

Macy stood in the shadows, dressed in her overalls and ragged shirt.

Her feet were bare. She picked up a cloth bundle and stuffed it under her arm. "I told you earlier I shouldn't be here," she said. "I gotta go." She swallowed. "Ty don't like it when I run off. I'll get it good if I don't show up tonight. Figured I'd borrow a horse an—"

"Borrow a horse?" Andi cut her off. "Don't you mean *steal* a horse?" The instant the words left her mouth, she regretted them. "I'm sorry, Macy. I didn't mean that. Why didn't you just ask?"

A flush crept up Macy's neck. "Nobody'd give the likes of me a horse to use." She narrowed her eyes. "Ain't that so?"

Andi said nothing. Macy was right. Chad's "no!" would have bounced off the ceiling.

"Got no choice but to help m'self." Macy raised her fist. "Get outta my way. You can't stop me."

"Are you that scared of your brothers?" Andi asked in a hushed voice. "You'd risk stealing a horse rather than spend the night away from them?"

Macy's fist fell limply to her side. Her face crumpled and a sob tore from her throat. She nodded.

"Stay here then," Andi blurted. "Don't go back at all. You can hide in our barn or stay in my room. They'd never find you. My brother's a lawyer. He could help." She didn't know how, but surely Justin could find a law somewhere about not beating up helpless girls.

Macy ran the back of her hand across her wet face and shook her head. "That's fool's talk. Ty'll find me. He always does. I took off once before, but I learned my lesson." She shuddered, lost in a memory Andi wanted no part of. When Macy's eyes refocused, she frowned. "Don't need no lawyer. I gotta go back."

"But *why*?"

"I told you. I got nobody else."

"You've got me," Andi said.

Macy ducked her head. "You don't know nothin' about it. How could you, a rich girl with a fine family?" She looked up and curled her fist once more. "I'm takin' a horse, ya hear? I'll leave it at the livery."

Macy's plight tugged at Andi's heart. She sounded desperate. What was the loan of one horse compared to her friend's terror? "All right. As long as you promise to—"

"Come out of there with your hands up!"

Andi's heart leaped to her throat. She and Macy stared at each other through the gloom. Macy clutched Andi's sleeve. "A-Andi . . ."

"Hurry up," the voice ordered from just outside the barn doors. "I got an itchy trigger finger."

Andi froze at the sound of a pistol's hammer pulling back.

"Maybe we can hide in a stall," Macy whispered.

"What good will that do?" Andi whispered back. "He'll just come in and find us. It's so dark that he might mistake us for horse thieves." *Which isn't too far from the truth*, she added silently.

"I'm countin' to three," the voice said. "Then I'm comin' in. One . . ."

Andi shuffled toward the barn entrance. Her legs felt like jelly.

"Two . . ."

She pushed open the heavy barn door and stepped out into the moonlight. At the sight of the dark figure and his weapon, her hands shot up. "Please don't shoot," she begged.

The man's jaw dropped. He jammed the gun back into his holster. Before he could say a word, another figure pushed forward. In seconds he had covered the distance between the pistol-wielding ranch hand and the girls.

"Mitch!" Andi nearly fainted in relief.

Her relief was short-lived. "What in blazes are you two doing out here?" Mitch yelled in a hoarse whisper. He gripped Andi's shoulders, making her wince. "Wyatt came near to mistaking you for a thief." He jerked his chin in the ranch hand's direction.

Wyatt looked sheepish. "Sorry, Miss Andi. I heard a clattering in the barn and voices, so I figured—"

Mitch whirled on him. "Don't apologize. You were doing your job." He turned back to Andi. "Answer me."

Andi exchanged a bleak look with Macy, who was shaking like a leaf. She couldn't come right out and say that her friend planned to help herself to a Carter horse. But anything else would be a lie. She scrambled to think of an answer. "Well . . ."

"It's m-my fault," Macy stuttered. "I g-got a hankerin' to get back to town, and Andi came lookin' for me. I—"

"Nobody would take her earlier," Andi jumped in. "Nobody gave her a chance to explain either. She's *got* to get back or her brothers will skin her alive. Can she take Pal?"

Mitch looked at Andi as if she'd lost her mind. "No." When she started to protest, he held up his hand. "For one thing, she needs more than a half-moon to see her way. For another, she's not familiar with the road."

"I'll grab a lantern and go with her."

"Let me finish," Mitch said. "I'm on my way out to join the crew near Stony Point. I reckon I could take the long way around and drop Macy close to town."

Macy sucked in her breath. "You'd do that?"

"I've met your brothers, remember? I don't want to give them any excuse to light into you." He turned to Wyatt. "Tell Chad I've been delayed." Then he grinned. "Just don't tell him why."

CHAPTER 20

The saying "clothes make the man" must be true even for girls. When Macy wore her new dress to school she behaved better. She only beat up one boy during the remainder of the term (and Jack deserved it). Now that school's out, Macy and I have all summer to work with my colts.

Andi wrapped her journal and stuffed it behind the feedbox in Taffy's stall. She'd been up at the crack of dawn to finish her chores early. Taffy's bedding was fresh, the other horses watered, and the sun had barely risen.

"I've got big plans today," she told her mare. "Right after breakfast we're going to take your babies out of the paddock and work on their ground manners." Sunny had lately decided he didn't want to be caught. It was a game to him. Andi knew Chad wouldn't put up with that for long.

Taffy whickered and nosed her oats.

"I hope Macy comes by today to give me a hand." Andi wrinkled her forehead in thought. She hadn't seen her friend for three days, which was odd. Macy lived and breathed for Sunny.

With school out, Macy rode over nearly every morning to help Andi with the colts. She had somehow managed to beg, borrow, or steal a scruffy-looking roan horse to make the trip. Andi didn't ask where it came from. With Chad too busy to work with her, Andi was glad for help any way she could get it, though Macy never stayed long. She was good with the colts. Even Sunny minded his manners around her. For all her rough-and-tumble ways, Macy showed nothing but careful kindness when it came to the cream twin.

"If you were as nice to people as you are to Sunny, you'd have plenty of friends," Andi had joked just the other day.

"Don't need plenty o' friends," Macy retorted, scowling. "I got *you*, don't I?"

Andi blinked to clear her head. If Macy came by this morning, wonderful. If not, Andi would have to recruit someone else's help. She straightened up and left the barn. Perhaps Melinda could be persuaded to lend a hand.

Five minutes later Andi pushed through the swinging door into the dining room. She stopped short. Her entire family sat in their usual places. She hadn't seen Chad or Mitch at breakfast for weeks. They usually snatched a bite to eat when they could and ate the rest of their meals at the chuck wagon out on the range. Justin had resumed working in town a couple of days a week, so he wasn't a breakfast stranger any longer, but the only meal the whole family ate together was supper.

A thrill shot through Andi. Perhaps their rustling worries were finally coming to an end. *It's about time!* Her family could take a break and celebrate the Fourth of July tomorrow. She got shivery thinking about the fireworks display, candy and lemonade, parades, horse races, and yes, even the long-winded speeches.

"Good morning," she said brightly. "Am I late?" She glanced at the clock. Six o'clock. No, she was definitely not late.

"You're right on time, sweetheart," Mother replied. "Sit down."

Only Melinda returned her "good morning." Her brothers ate in silence.

They're probably bone-tired, Andi decided when not even Justin greeted her. She helped herself to a small stack of hotcakes and plopped them onto her plate. Without a word, Mitch slid the syrup pitcher across the table.

"Thanks," she said and poured a flood of maple syrup over the pancakes.

She said a quick blessing, cut into her stack, and lifted a forkful halfway to her mouth. "Say, Melinda, how would you like to help me with the colts this morning?" She popped the bite into her mouth and waited.

"I thought Macy was your colts' constant companion," Melinda said.

Andi shrugged. "She hasn't shown up lately, and I really need the help today. What do you say?"

"I would like to but . . ." Melinda flicked an uncertain glance at their mother.

"Melinda has already promised to help Mrs. Reid with one of her projects for the Ladies' Aid," Elizabeth said.

"Too bad," Andi replied. She looked at Chad. He was focusing all his attention on his meal. "Does eating breakfast with us mean things are settling down around here? I hope so. Can you take a little time off and help me with—"

"'Fraid not," Chad mumbled through a mouthful. "Not today."

"Mitch? Want to help? Or are you too busy getting ready for the big race tomorrow?" She grinned. Chase was the fastest horse in the valley.

"I'm not racing this year, or even going to the celebration." He looked disappointed. "Too much happening around here."

Andi slumped. *Rustlers sure know how to ruin a holiday.* Then she brightened. "Maybe I can ride Taffy in your place. After all, what's a Fourth of July race without a Carter winning it?"

"No, Andrea," Mother said.

Andi sighed. Mother had put a stop to racing in public two years ago, after she caught her daughter winning the Fourth of July race. *No Carter will be racing tomorrow? Cory and Flash will win for sure!*

There was no use arguing. She let it go and turned to Justin. "I expect you're mighty tired of playing rancher with Chad. Could you take a break and come see my colts? I'll show you everything Macy and I have taught them."

"I'd like nothing better," Justin said. "But I have a backlog of paperwork in town that I can't put off any longer. I'm sorry."

Andi shrugged. "That's all right. Just thought I'd ask."

The silence grew. Andi dug into her breakfast, disappointed. No Fourth of July celebration. No help with the colts. No cheerful mealtime chatter. Why did everyone look so gloomy? "Well, maybe I'll saddle Taffy and take the colts for a run. They can always use more practice getting used to creeks and flapping branches, right?"

No one answered. Andi finished her breakfast in a hurry. *It's no fun sitting around a table of sour faces.* "May I be excused?"

Elizabeth nodded.

Chad cleared his throat. "Now that you've finished eating, I need a word with you."

The room crackled with tension. *What now?* Andi mentally ran through her list of chores and did not find herself lacking. She stood up and shoved her chair in. "Too late, big brother. Mother excused me." She stepped away from the table.

"Sit down."

Elizabeth sighed, as if she'd suddenly changed her mind about something. "Let her go, Chad."

"Mother," Chad said in a low voice, "what good does it do putting off—"

"I'll be outside with the colts," Andi said. "You can talk to me all you want out there. Afterward"—she smiled—"maybe I can talk you into helping me."

Before anyone could call her back, Andi hurried from the dining room, through the kitchen, and onto the porch. She made a quick stop at the outdoor pump to wash the rest of the syrup from her face then straightened up. It was a lovely summer morning. Andi wasted no time heading for the paddock.

She whistled for the colts. When she heard no answering nickers or galloping hooves, she climbed to the top of the fence and hollered, "Sunny! Shasta!"

No response.

Andi shaded her eyes against the early morning sun. It rose above the foothills, making her squint. Her gaze swept the large enclosure. Perhaps the colts were clear past the trees, near the irrigation ditch. She wouldn't be able to see them, but they would surely hear her whistle. Even if Shasta or Sunny didn't hear it, the others would respond. Never had they missed her call.

"Where are you?" Andi yelled at the top of her voice.

A minute later, a number of colts and fillies came galloping into sight and up to the fence. As usual, they shoved and nipped to get Andi's attention. She scratched their noses and craned her neck to see around the frisky group. Shasta and Sunny were nowhere in sight. Neither was Apache or the black fillies. A few others were missing too.

Confused and unhappy, Andi dropped down from the railing. "Maybe there's a break in the fence. I better tell Chad before they all get out."

She took two steps away from the paddock and collided with Chad. "Where are my colts?" she asked. "I've whistled and called, but Shasta and Sunny don't answer. Only these." She waved toward the horses. "Did the others get out? Is there a break in the fence?"

"Well . . . yes and no."

Andi frowned. "What does that mean—yes or no? Did you put them out on the range? You said they'd be better off in the near paddock, what with the rustlers and all. Did you stable them for safekeeping? Why didn't you tell me?"

Dumb question. When it came to running the ranch, Chad did not consult his youngest sister. He did what he thought best. "Is that what you wanted to tell me at breakfast? That Shasta and Sunny are in the barn? I didn't see them there this morning." She took a breath to ply him with more questions.

"Are you finished?"

Andi fell silent. She was *not* finished, but something in Chad's voice stopped her cold. She glanced back at the half-empty paddock then looked at her brother. His expression said it all. A sudden chill gripped her. "Chad? Where—"

"They're gone."

Andi felt her world flip upside down. She didn't believe it. She *couldn't* believe it. "You're wrong. They're here somewhere."

Chad sagged against the fence. "No, Andi, they're not. Mitch found a break in the southeast fence early this morning. It looks like a deliberate break. We didn't want to ruin your breakfast, so I waited until . . ." He took a deep breath and straightened. "There's no good way to break news like this."

Andi tried to swallow the lump that clogged her throat. It didn't work. Tears pricked her eyes. "You mean they've been rustled? Like the cattle?"

Chad nodded. "Yes, along with ten other colts. McLaughlin lost three yearlings, so we've been extra watchful. When no more horses went missing from any of the ranchers, we figured the rustlers had changed their minds about trying for horses. But—"

"You can get them back, right?" Andi broke in. Of course he could! "You *have* to."

"If I knew where they were, I would have gone after them already," Chad stormed. "And if I knew where the rustlers were keeping our beef, I'd get *them* back too!" He slammed his palm against the fence post.

Andi flinched. Too many nights without sleep had turned Chad into a shadow of his usual self. Dark circles stood out under his eyes. He looked close to his wit's end. "I'm sorry," he mumbled. "I didn't mean to snap at you."

Andi barely nodded. Her insides were too busy catching on fire. "How dare those rustlers steal my colts!" She sprinted for the barn.

"Hey!" Chad caught up to her just outside the doors and grabbed her arm. "What are you up to?"

"I'm going after my colts." She tried to peel Chad's fingers away from her arm. "Let me go."

"Now it's your turn to simmer down, little sister." He kept a firm but gentle grip on her arm. "You can help best by staying out of our way. Let Mitch and me take care of this problem."

Andi stopped tearing at her brother's fingers and turned tearful eyes on him. "Promise me you'll find my colts."

Chad opened his mouth to reply, then shut it and slowly shook his head. "You know I can't promise that. McLaughlin never recovered his ponies, and it's been four weeks. They're most likely sold and out of the state by now."

Andi felt sick. She burst into tears. "I want my colts."

"I know." Chad pulled Andi around and drew her into his arms. "Go ahead and cry all you want." He held her close.

Andi wept until she had no tears left. Her face felt hot and swollen. Hiccupping and sniffing, she accepted Chad's bandana and blew her nose.

"Feel better?" Chad kept his arm around her and led her toward the house.

"No."

Crying had not made Andi feel better. Nothing would ever make her feel better. How could it, when Shasta and Sunny were gone?

CHAPTER 21

I feel like I'm bouncing around on the back of a bucking bronco. Up one second; down the next. Trouble is, I can't figure out a way to stop this ride and get off without getting hurt.

Andi was saddling Taffy when she heard Macy call her name. She sighed. *I don't want to talk to anybody, especially not to Macy.* The whole day had turned into one colossal misery, ever since her early morning discovery of the missing colts. It was only because her mother insisted she go for a ride that Andi found herself in the barn readying her horse.

"We'll ride up to our special spot," she told Taffy and led her outside. She hoped it was far away from any rustler mischief. Last time she'd checked, the creek was running full. She ducked back into the barn to collect her pole and bait bucket.

"Andi!"

Macy's shrill call pulled Andi away from her task. She left the fishing gear where she found it and poked her head out between the wide double doors.

"Didn't ya hear me hollerin'?" Macy trotted across the yard. The roan horse looked worn out. Macy didn't appear much better. She was back in her overalls, which needed a good washing. So did she. Pale hair hung limply around her dirty face; her eyes were red rimmed and puffy.

"I heard you," Andi answered with no enthusiasm. "We can't work with the colts today because . . ." She stopped and bit her lip.

"Because they ain't here," Macy finished. Her shoulders slumped.

Andi froze. "How did you know?"

Macy swept a wary gaze around the yard. Ranch hands were going about their work. "Can't tell you here." She yanked on the reins and took off toward a small grove of trees in the distance.

Andi clambered up onto Taffy and galloped after Macy. A minute later she pulled up alongside her friend and slowed the mare to a walk. They were alone, yet Macy turned her horse in a full circle and carefully scanned the area before stopping.

"Why are you so jittery?" Andi demanded. "What are you afraid of?"

Macy dismounted and tied the roan to an old oak. Then she collapsed on the ground and let out a piercing wail.

Prickles raced up and down Andi's neck at the eerie sound. She slid off Taffy and fell beside Macy. "What's the matter?" Her heart thudded at the evil possibilities. "Did your brothers beat you?"

Macy shook her head wildly. "No, n-nothin' like that. Leastways, not t'day." She sat up and caught Andi's shoulders. Taking a deep breath, she blurted, "I gotta tell you somethin', and you can't never tell nobody. Not *ever*."

"What are you talking about?"

"Promise!"

"Why?"

"I . . ." Macy let Andi go and sat back on the grass. "I know where your colts are. I seen 'em."

Andi gasped. *"Where?"* She thrust her face close to Macy's. "Tell me."

Macy shook her head. "You gotta promise first. If you don't, I'm gonna mount up an' ride outta here. You'll never see them colts again." Her expression grew hard.

Andi shivered. Whatever Macy wanted to tell her, she seemed terrified that somebody would find out. But a *promise*? A promise was not something to be considered lightly. How many times had she seen her brothers seal a transaction with nothing more than a word and a handshake? "A man's word is his bond," Chad often said. If Andi gave her word to Macy, she would have to keep it, whatever the cost.

From the look on Macy's face, the cost of keeping this promise might run high.

"Do you promise?" Macy asked again. Her eyes pleaded.

Andi pondered. *If it's the only way I can find out where Shasta and Sunny are, then . . .* "Yes," she agreed before she could change her mind.

Macy let out a breath that ended in a sob. "Oh, Andi, thank you! I'm glad. I need your help. Poor Sunny's pinin' for home."

"Tell me where they are."

Macy's voice dropped to a whisper. "Rock Canyon."

"Rock Canyon?" Andi shook her head in disbelief. "Nobody's fool enough to keep anything there. The canyon walls are always eroding, throwing rocks and dirt to the floor. The entrance isn't wide enough to run a team of horses through."

"You're right about *that*," Macy agreed. "You been there?"

Andi nodded. "Cory and I explored it once. But we got out fast when we heard a rockslide. Ever since then we ride past without stopping."

"You're smart to stay out," Macy agreed. "It's an evil place." She blew out a breath. "But that's where your colts are."

"How did you find them? What were you doing way out there in that risky place?"

Macy didn't answer.

"Macy," Andi tried again. "Why would you—"

"My brothers put 'em there." Her face crumpled. "It's where they're holdin' the livestock before they move 'em out to sell."

"What?" Andi reeled backward in shock and revulsion.

Macy choked back a sob. "Andi, don't look at me like that."

"Your *brothers* are the cattle rustlers?"

Macy nodded. "I don't want no part of it, but they make me help watch the stock." She closed her eyes and shuddered. "They got a bunch of irons they use to change over the brands. I seen 'em. And not just *your* beef. I saw Rockin' R and Bent Pine livestock too. But I never saw no horses . . . not 'til this mornin'."

Macy looked up. Sick fear filled her eyes. "Does the law hang *girls?*"

Andi didn't know. Probably not. But she couldn't answer. Her world was spinning out of control. She swallowed to keep her breakfast where it belonged.

Macy started crying. "I tried to talk 'em outta this fool notion, but Ty thrashed me and promised more of the same if I didn't do my part. 'If folks can't look out for their stock, they don't deserve to keep 'em,'" she recited bleakly. "That's the Walker brothers' motto. Ty says it's mine too."

She ran the back of her hand across her dripping nose. "But it *ain't* mine. Not no more. Not since I met *you.* You and your family are real Christian-like. Ain't never seen no family treat each other so fine." Another torrent of tears fell. "But me? I ain't nothin' but a slave, just like one of them luckless black folks before the War. Only I'm worse off. Ain't nobody gonna fight a war to free *me.*"

Andi let Macy cry awhile longer. Then she took a deep breath and said, "You can be free, Macy. Tell the sheriff or my brothers—"

"I can't!" Macy howled. "I'm in it as deep as they are. Besides, Ty told me just this mornin' that we're through here. He wants to get outta the valley before the ranchers close in. Soon as they change these colts' brands they're movin' 'em out—probably tomorrow—along with the last of the beef. Then we'll disappear."

"Tomorrow?" Andi felt the blood drain from her face. She rose. "I've got to tell—"

"No!" Macy yanked Andi down beside her. "You can't tell nobody. You promised. I rode all the way over here to tell you how to get Shasta and Sunny back. But you gotta do it tonight. By tomorrow night we'll be gone. Nobody gets hurt, and the rustlin's done with. Ain't that what the ranchers want?"

Andi's throat felt too tight to say anything. She didn't know about the other ranchers, but Chad didn't just want the rustling to stop. He wanted to catch those responsible, give them a speedy trial, and get right to the hanging.

I have to tell him. It was the sensible thing to do. If she told, however, she would break her word to Macy. Macy, who had not only entrusted Andi with her dangerous secret but had also poured out her heart. *Can I turn on her just to catch a couple of cattle thieves?* So far, none of the ranchers or their hired help had been hurt or killed. In a day or two, the rustlers would be gone.

"Ain't lettin' us go worth the price of getting Shasta and Sunny back?" Macy pleaded. "I took a big chance tellin' you. I kept quiet when it was just cows, but I like you, Andi. You been good to me. I couldn't keep quiet about your colts."

Andi swallowed the ache in her throat and nervously fingered the ends of her braids. Macy had indeed risked a lot by coming here. "So," she whispered, "how do I get my colts back?"

Macy scooted closer. "Poor things are skittish. They're bunched together in a makeshift corral next to the canyon wall. They don't like it in the canyon, and I don't blame 'em. All night I hear rocks and boulders fallin'. They crack like gunshots. Scares me half to death." She smiled suddenly. "When Sunny saw me he settled right down. I whispered in his ear that I'd get him and Shasta outta this fix." She paused.

"Go on," Andi said. "I'm still waiting to hear the plan."

"Me and Rudy are watchin' the livestock. Ty and Jase moved half the steers out this mornin'. They won't be back 'til late tonight. Right now Rudy's drunk as a skunk and sleepin' it off. I snuck past him to find you. But I gotta get back soon."

Macy took a deep breath. "Anyways, it's gotta be you who comes for the colts. I can't disappear with 'em. Rudy may be drunk, but he ain't stupid. He'll near kill me if I try to take them colts outta the canyon." She shivered. "If you come before midnight, I'll keep Rudy busy. I'll make enough noise to hide any sounds the colts make."

Andi pressed her lips together and thought hard. So far, it didn't sound too bad.

"You go to the canyon, grab your colts, and get outta there quick as you can," Macy finished. "In the morning they'll notice a couple missin' colts, but they won't blame me—not with Rudy and me together all night. I'll get thrashed for not watchin' careful, but I can stand it if I know the colts are safe. You gotta hide 'em for a day while we get away. Then you can tell your brothers whatever you like."

"I thought you made me promise *never* to tell."

"Once we're gone, I don't care," Macy relented with a shrug.

Andi's stomach churned. Rock Canyon was a long way—a good hour's ride into the hills. She could find it with no trouble; the full moon would light her way brighter than ten lanterns. *But do I want to go into that death trap, especially at night?*

"Can you do it?" Macy asked when Andi kept silent. "Can you get Sunny outta the canyon without gettin' caught?"

"Yes," Andi said. That was the easy part. She would be riding Taffy. Sunny and Shasta would follow their mother anywhere. The hard part— the part she didn't tell Macy—was rescuing the rest of the colts. She'd given Macy no promise about taking just the two weanlings. *No dirty horse thieves will sell any Carter colts*, she silently vowed.

"Good." Macy gave Andi a nervous grin. "You know what? This is the scariest thing I ever done—deceive my brothers like this. But I love Sunny and can't stand for him to be sold to strangers." She blew out a sad breath. "And they'd never let *me* keep him."

Andi clasped her hands together to keep them from trembling. "This is going to be one of the scariest things I've ever done too."

"Andi?" Macy whispered. "I was wonderin' if . . . well . . ." She cleared her throat and looked up. Her cheeks showed two red spots. "Do you think you could say a prayer or somethin'? I'm mighty scared."

Andi's eyes opened wide in surprise. Macy wanted a prayer? Macy the roughneck who less than a month ago had nearly been the cause of Andi's death? *Incredible.* Andi didn't know quite how to pray, especially with that dangerous promise hanging over her head, but she did her best to ask God for the one thing they both needed right now: peace.

CHAPTER 22

*Tonight I'm going out to Rock Canyon to rescue
Shasta and Sunny . . . Macy's brothers are the
rustlers . . . Never in my life have I wanted to
break a promise more than I want to right now.
I'm scared.*

Andi felt better after she wrote it all down. She closed her journal and carefully wrapped it in a length of wool felt. Instead of wedging it behind Taffy's feedbox, she held onto it. "Melinda's right," she said softly. "A journal is a good place to share thoughts I only want God and me to know about."

Andi had not told her family the rustlers' identities, although her decision to keep her word to Macy weighed heavily on her heart. Twice during supper she had almost blurted out her discovery. Her brothers looked so worn out. "I could have solved their troubles with only a few sentences," she told Taffy. "Instead, I asked Mother if I could spend the night out here."

Andi was astonished at how quickly her mother had agreed. Everybody thought it was a good idea. They most likely assumed she was fretting over her colts. "I am," she said, cinching up Taffy's saddle. "But not as much as I'm worried about where I'm headed tonight."

Andi led Taffy out of her stall. She closed the half door and for the first time ever placed her journal in its felt wrapping in plain sight on the ledge. If all went well, she would return the bundle to its hiding place well before morning. If things did not go well . . .

A feeling of being tugged like a wishbone tore at Andi's insides. Which half would win? Andi hoped a journal entry did not count as breaking a promise, but this time she would not disappear without an explanation.

It was well past sunset when Andi headed out. She didn't worry about being seen. Her brothers and the ranch hands had vanished shortly after supper for another night of trying to root out the cattle thieves. *You're looking in the wrong place!* she'd wanted to shout.

A huge white disk rose over the Sierra Nevada, lighting the east road as brightly as if it were daytime. Andi urged Taffy into a steady, swinging lope. Her horse bounded forward, eager to be off on an evening ride with her mistress. The July night was warm and pleasant. Andi listened to the *clippety-clop* of Taffy's hooves and her easy breathing and relaxed.

She had plenty of time to think about her destination. The small box canyon was a splendid place to keep livestock. A thief only needed to block the narrow entrance and the entire canyon became a corral. During her one-and-only visit, Andi had seen clumps of stunted aspen, cotton-wood, and willows clinging to life in the narrow, sun-starved canyon. She and Cory had watered their horses at the boggy spring. They agreed it was a perfect hidden canyon but far too hazardous to spend time there.

Macy's brothers were proving smarter than they looked. They had rightly figured that no rancher would consider Rock Canyon a potential hideaway. It was a tiny, out-of-the-way crack in thousands of square acres of hills and valleys. Not even desperate, low-down rustlers would risk their lives for a bunch of stolen steers.

"Oh, yes, they would," Andi said and slowed Taffy for a much-needed rest.

The evening slipped by. The moon rose higher. Andi plodded on into the foothills. Straight ahead, the canyon's cliffs rose like sentries, mark-ing the entrance. The jagged rocks were hard to miss. The way ahead cut through oaks and manzanita, with a few scattered pines. Trampled scrub brush and churned-up grass marked the passing of stolen cattle.

Andi stopped for a final rest. In spite of the warm night, she shivered. The canyon would be much cooler than out in the open. Dark too, unless the moon rose above the cliffs. She patted Taffy. "Let's go, girl. In and out."

Taffy snorted and headed straight for the canyon entrance. The narrow path wound its way around huge boulders and over the top of small stones. Andi led her horse carefully past debris from previous rockslides, staying as close to the center of the trail as possible. She couldn't guess how the cattle made it in and out through this gap without bringing the walls down.

A sound like a handful of marbles being tossed down stairs brought Andi to a halt. "It's all right." She leaned over to rub Taffy's neck. "Just a bit of rubble." She glanced up and prayed that tonight there would be no sudden wind or rainstorm to loosen more debris and bring it down on her head.

Taffy snorted and continued on her way. A minute later, the mare sidestepped without warning. Andi clutched the reins. "Easy, girl." She strained to see along the gloomy path. What had startled Taffy? Then she smelled it. "Phew. What is that awful stink?"

Taffy whinnied nervously and tried to bolt, but Andi held her in check. Two dark, swollen mounds to the left caught her eye. "Oh, no!" She choked back her nausea at the odor of rotting flesh. Some of the stolen livestock had not been so lucky. They lay dead and abandoned, victims of a hail of stones from above.

Andi hurried Taffy past the grisly scene. She did not want to see any brand marks. It was best to keep her mind on the task at hand and not mourn for the animals' cruel death and the waste of good beef.

The narrow way opened onto the wider floor of the canyon. It appeared clear of the worst of the debris. The moon's pale glow from behind the cliffs revealed scrub brush and small trees. In the distance, a yellow light shone from a black, square shape. Andi hoped Macy was inside and ready to do her part.

The canyon was filled with night noises. Crickets and frogs called from the brush and faraway spring. The faint lowing of cattle mingled with the rattle of falling rubble. Andi's stomach tightened. Some of those bawling steers probably belonged to her family. "I am not here to rescue cows," she whispered and moved on.

A few minutes later she found what she was looking for. Someone had constructed a crude corral a number of yards past the shack. Andi was certain the colts inside recognized her and Taffy. They clumped against the railing, heads up, alert, and not making a sound. Above the enclosure, a rocky overhang kept the weather off them but also threatened to break loose at any moment. *How can the rustlers keep such valuable colts in danger like this?* A flush of anger swept through Andi clear to her toes, banishing her fear.

Shasta nickered a low greeting. Andi caught her breath. She dismounted and hurried over. "Shhh." She laid her hand over Shasta's nose. "Keep quiet, all of you."

Just then, a loud clattering erupted from the shack. A man snarled a curse, and Macy shouted back. Andi didn't know how long Macy could argue with her brother and slam things around. The horses jostled each other and crowded up against the rough-hewn pine logs that served as railings. Andi could see they did not like the noise. They wanted out *right now.*

Hurry, hurry! Andi slipped the coiled rope from her saddle horn. Then she took a deep breath. This had to be done just right. The colts were already skittish. If she didn't lasso Apache on the first throw, he would startle even more. The rest would scatter and make enough noise to bring Macy's brother running.

Andi licked her dry, chapped lips and lifted the rope latch from around the post. The gate swung inward. She opened it all the way and stepped inside the small corral. As quietly as she could, Andi loosened her lasso and swung it in circles above her head, feeling for the rhythm. It was one skill even Chad admitted Andi had mastered. "Must be all those dogs you lassoed when you were little," he often teased.

There was no teasing tonight, not even in her thoughts. Her first throw had to count.

When the lasso began to twirl, the young horses left the railing and bunched together in a corner. Most times, Andi liked to circle the group and pick out her target after careful consideration. Not tonight. She was in a hurry and she already knew her target.

Apache turned toward her. Andi let her loop fly. It settled smoothly around the paint's neck, and she tightened it with a quick yank. Apache snorted, but he gave no other sign of being ruffled.

Andi relaxed. *I sure wish Chad could have seen that throw.* She led the paint colt out of the corral and mounted Taffy. Once firmly settled in the saddle, she nudged her mare and gave Apache's rope a tug. He responded instantly.

Free at last, the remaining colts rushed through the corral gate. Sunny and Shasta bounded ahead and crowded close to their mother. "It won't be long now," she assured them. She led Apache toward the entrance of the canyon. The rest followed, and Andi began to breathe easier. Everything was working exactly as she and Macy had planned. She would soon be home. Tomorrow, Macy and her lawless brothers would be long gone from the valley. *Good riddance!*

Once Andi was well away from the shack, she picked up the pace. She glanced to her left, where Sunny trotted alongside her. "Macy did this for you, you know. She loves you a lot. I bet she's really going to miss you." *I'll miss Macy too*, Andi thought. *If I hadn't befriended her, Shasta and Sunny would be long gone.* Her chest swelled in gratitude.

The colts turned restless when they passed the bloated carcasses, but Andi soft-talked Apache and tugged on his lead rope. They reached the last leg of their flight to freedom with no mishaps. Andi brought Taffy to a halt, and Apache stopped too. The rest followed suit. Andi did a quick head count in the gloom. The horses waited impatiently, pawing the ground and shuffling. Up ahead, rocks bounced and clattered down the canyon walls.

Andi couldn't predict when a rock or a boulder might dislodge up above and tumble down, knocking out other stones in its wake. She did know that crowding a dozen skittish horses through the narrow gap ahead was a recipe for disaster. They would have to go through single file.

She looked at her charges. Shasta and Sunny flanked Taffy, bumping against Andi's legs. The other horses stood clumped together in twos and threes. "I can't lead each of you through one by one." More rubble fell. A horse whinnied.

Regret colored Andi's thoughts. Fear followed. "I shouldn't have taken you all," she said. Once the horses started through, there was a good chance they would panic. They were already nervous, and no colt wanted to be left behind.

Shasta's frightened nicker triggered Andi's decision. Right now it was Shasta and Sunny who counted. She would have to leave the rest of the colts behind to fend for themselves, no matter how much she hated to do it.

Suddenly, two colts squealed. Andi whirled. A black and a sorrel had been pushed against the canyon wall. They scuffled with each other, trying to make room. Pebbles and small rocks fell from above and bounced off their backs, startling the colts even more. Two others wedged forward, knocking into Taffy. She snorted.

The sound of falling debris grew louder. A jumble of fist-sized stones tumbled down around them. *This is bad!* Andi let go of Apache's rope and covered her head. A rock hit her arm. "Go, Taffy!" She jammed her heels into the mare's sides. Taffy leaped forward.

Just behind Andi, more rubble spilled. The colts screamed. Like a river with no outlet, the young horses surged against Taffy. Shasta and Sunny leaped ahead of the group and galloped through the gap to freedom.

Andi ducked. A rock missed her and hit Taffy on the rump. The mare whinnied and swerved to the side, slamming Andi against the canyon wall. Sharp rocks scraped across her arm and leg. She yelped. Taffy kept running. Apache nosed his way forward and forced himself past the horse and rider, frantic to escape.

Dirt and small pebbles rained down. Andi threw one arm over her head, gripped the reins, and hunkered down to ride it out. It was no use. The colts' mad dash and the cascade of dirt threw Andi into confusion. She couldn't see anything in the dark and she couldn't breathe through her dust-filled nostrils.

Just as the gap widened, more rocks and dirt fell. Taffy stumbled and made a sharp turn. Andi flew from the saddle and crashed onto a pile of rubble. Other horses thundered past and disappeared into the night.

CHAPTER 23

I can't find words to describe how much I hurt.

Sharp, shooting pain brought Andi to her senses. She came to with a cry that ripped the night air. She didn't care who heard her. Probably nobody could, not with the last of the rock shower still settling in the distance. She squeezed her eyes shut and thanked God she'd missed the worst of the falling debris.

A pain-filled whinny close by brought Andi around. One of the colts had not fared well. Head drooping and favoring his left foreleg, the young bay horse limped past. "At least you can still walk," Andi said through clenched teeth. She couldn't walk. She couldn't move. Her sleeve felt sticky with blood from where she'd scraped the rocky wall. Her head pounded, and her shoulder throbbed.

And her foot? It burned like a red-hot branding iron. She'd accidentally touched an iron once, and it hurt just like this. Except this fire came from deep inside and couldn't be relieved by dousing it with cold water. The searing pain made her other scrapes and bruises seem petty.

Forcing herself not to cry out again, Andi took a deep breath and slowly pushed herself up. Her ankle screamed. She blinked back tears and looked around. She sat just outside the black mouth of the canyon's entrance. Overhead, the moon glowed a harsh white.

In the canyon a large boulder crashed to the ground. The loud *crack* echoed through the gap. Andi winced. *A few more yards and those rocks would be falling on me.* Fear for Shasta and Sunny made her yell, "Taffy!"

Like magic, Taffy trotted out of the shadows with the foals at her side. She whickered and nuzzled Andi's hair. Andi reached up and buried her head in Taffy's soft neck. Huge sobs burst from her throat. "I'm so sorry," she blubbered. Instead of rescuing her colts, she'd nearly killed them.

Andi wanted to keep Taffy and the colts close during the long, miserable night ahead, but she had to send them home. Nobody knew she was out here. Nobody would look for her until morning. Then *maybe* someone would go to fetch her from the barn for breakfast. *Maybe* they would see her journal lying in plain view. *Maybe* somebody would read it.

"Too many maybes," Andi said. Worse, she had to be gone from this place by midnight, before Macy's brothers returned. The way she felt, she wasn't going anywhere. She drew a deep breath and tugged on Taffy's reins.

The mare lowered her head.

"Go home," Andi ordered.

Taffy tossed her head and blew out. She pawed the ground, kicking rocks away.

"I know you want me to come, but I can't. You have to go home."

Taffy stood over Andi like a sentinel. She didn't move. In the moonlight, Shasta and Sunny quivered with uncertainty. "I did all this to rescue your babies," Andi said. "You have to go." She glanced around. A dead branch lay just beyond her reach. Struggling against the burning in her ankle and the rest of her injuries, she scooted across the ground and picked up the stick. "I'm sorry, girl." She pulled herself up on one knee and smacked Taffy smartly on the rump. "Go home!"

Taffy snorted her surprise and galloped off in the direction of the ranch. The twins shadowed their mother. "Please, God," Andi whispered while she watched the vanishing horses. "See them safely back to the ranch."

There was nothing to do now but wait. Andi wrapped her arms around the knee of her good leg and buried her head in them. Her foot continued to throb and burn. She tried to pray, but no words came. She hurt too much. Tonight she would have to trust God to read her heart and know what she wanted to say.

It felt like hours, but only a few minutes passed before voices broke the still night air. Andi perked up and listened.

"I *saw* it, Ty. Not more'n a couple hundred yards yonder," a nasal voice insisted.

Ty laughed. "You're drunk and seein' things, Jase. No time to chase ghosts."

"I ain't drunk. Leastways not much." Jase swore. "See that? A horse with a rope 'round its neck. I'm goin' after it."

"Not now," Ty snapped. "You'll break your fool neck. C'mon. Here's the entrance."

Andi huddled motionless against the rubble. She prayed the men would continue on their way without seeing her. It could work. Covered in grit and dust, she looked like a small boulder. If she held especially still—

"What in tarnation happened here?"

The men pulled their horses to a stop, dumbstruck. Andi lay so close she could see their shocked expressions as they surveyed the results of the rockslide. A sudden movement brought their pistols up. When the lame bay colt hobbled toward them, Ty put away his gun. "We got that batch o' steers out just in time," he said. "This place ain't safe. Glad we're clearin' out."

"How we gonna get the rest of the stock out?"

Ty shrugged. "We'll figure a way. If not we'll leave 'em. Though I hate t' leave them pretty little colts."

Too late, Andi thought with grim satisfaction. *They're long gone by now, except that poor bay.* It was hard to keep still, but she dared not move a finger. Rocks don't move. If she twitched, they'd find her.

"Let's see how bad it's blocked," Jase finally said.

Before the men had gone ten feet, a horse and rider emerged from the canyon's gaping blackness. "Ty! Jase!" The rider called out and held up the lantern he was carrying. Another horse appeared carrying Macy.

"Rudy!" Ty shouted. "What's goin' on here?"

Rudy galloped up and yanked his gelding to a bone-jarring stop. In the moonlight, his face looked red with rage. It matched his wild hair and beard exactly. "Somebody set the colts loose." He gave Macy a dirty look. She cowered on the back of the roan horse. "We rounded up two of 'em, but the rest got out."

"That explains the roped horse I saw," Jase muttered.

Ty swore. "Did you catch who done it?"

Rudy shook his head. "It took time comin' through the gap. It's a mess." As if to reinforce the danger, another shower of dirt and rocks fell close by. Rudy's horse shied nervously. The man sawed at his mount's mouth. The horse reared and came down barely a stone's throw from where Andi crouched.

"What the—" He broke off and gaped at the filthy figure in the rubble. Andi stared back.

At Rudy's outcry, the others gathered around. When Macy saw Andi, her eyes and mouth opened wide. An instant later, a mask of indifference fell over her face. She turned away.

Jase dropped from his horse. "Now, ain't this interestin'." He squatted next to Andi and grabbed her chin. "I seen you before, girl." He shot Macy a dangerous look. "With *you*."

Macy threw back her shoulders. "She ain't no friend o' mine."

"Mighty peculiar," Rudy put in. He scratched his beard and squinted. "This here looks like the same girl you was too yellow to fight." When Macy didn't answer, he yanked her from the horse and shook her. "Answer me." A blow sent her sprawling.

Macy staggered to her feet breathing hard. "Yeah." She clenched her fists. "I know better now," she finally said.

"I bet this girl freed the colts," Jase said. His dark brows drew together.

He stood and turned on his sister. "How d'ya reckon she knew where to find 'em?"

Macy's face turned paper white, but she answered boldly. "Don't go pinnin' this on me, Jase. How would I know?"

Ty shoved his way to the forefront and took over. "Enough! It don't matter. We're gettin' outta here." He flicked an uneasy glance at Andi. "But not before we get rid of the girl."

"Hey!" Macy hollered.

"Hey *what*?" Ty demanded.

"What d'ya mean *get rid* of her?" Macy sounded cocky, but Andi knew she must be frightened half out of her wits. "Ya mean *kill* her?"

"What else?" Rudy shot back. "If she tells what she's seen, the law'll be on us quicker than a duck on a June bug."

Macy licked her lips and shrugged. "Sure. All right. But . . ." Her eyes showed a sudden gleam. "Maybe there's another way. She's worth heaps o' money." She turned to Ty. "Might make up for losing the colts."

Silence.

Andi watched, shivering with horror. She sure hoped Macy knew what she was doing. *Please, Lord, keep them greedy.*

Jase looked skeptical. "What makes her so valuable? She don't look like much t' me."

"That's all *you* know," Macy snapped. "Her family owns the spread where y'all got them fine-lookin' ponies. Her name's Carter."

"What?" All three men started. An ugly smile split Rudy's beard. "Appears you been busy makin' friends from the other side o' the tracks, Macy-girl."

"She ain't my friend!" Macy insisted through clenched teeth. "Just thought ya shouldn't be in such a hurry to get rid of her."

Ty grunted his agreement. "Mebbe so. Might be good money in this scheme. It's worth considerin'. So long as she don't give us no trouble." An instant later he scooped Andi up and tossed her on his horse. "Let's head back."

Andi gasped at the man's rough treatment but uttered no cry. *Be quiet. Don't be any trouble*, she told herself.

Ty kept a tight hold around Andi's waist and nudged his horse. "You hurtin'? Good. That oughta keep ya in one place." He picked his way carefully over the rockslide debris. It was difficult to see by the light of the faint lantern. The horses stumbled and lurched through the dark gap. Andi hung on and prayed.

"This is worse than I thought," Ty growled to the others. "We'll never drive that beef through here now."

When they reached the cabin, Andi heard a whinny. The two recaptured colts paced the crude corral. They seemed frantic to escape. Andi sympathized with their plight. Her eyes smarted with unshed tears. She was just as trapped and frightened as the two young horses.

CHAPTER 24

Writing journal pages in my head was one way to keep from going crazy with fear. Another way was remembering Bible verses. And praying.

Ty carried Andi across the threshold and into the drafty cabin. It was a dark, dismal place, worse even than the shack Andi and her friends had shared last summer when they were stranded in the Sierras.

The others crowded in behind Ty. Rudy set the lantern on the table and kicked the front door closed. The shack shook. Across the room, the back door stood open a crack. Dust blew in. The lantern's glow showed a fireplace's dead ashes, a few straight-back chairs, and some bedrolls thrown haphazardly in the corners. Boxes of food stuffs lined one wall.

Andi had never seen a worse-stocked place in her life. The only items in good supply were the full and half-empty whiskey bottles. They were scattered everywhere. Broken glass littered the floor.

Ty crossed the room in a dozen steps and dumped Andi in a corner by the drafty back door. He slammed the door shut, but a *squeak* told Andi the door had no intention of obeying Ty. It slid back to its original position. More dust swirled.

Andi clamped her jaw hard to keep from screaming. The pain in her ankle had grown worse. Her foot was swelling badly. She reached for her boot and gave it an experimental tug. Fresh pain shot up her leg. She whimpered.

Before she could try again, Ty dragged Macy over and flung her down beside Andi. "Make sure she stays put." He turned his back on the girls, grabbed a bottle of whiskey, and joined his brothers at the table.

"Like she's goin' anywhere with a bum foot?" Macy mocked.

The men ignored her.

Macy put her mouth to Andi's ear. "I *told* you to be careful and get it done quick. What happened? How did all them colts get loose?"

"I'm sorry," Andi mouthed, and shook her head. She winced and sucked in a breath. "My ankle really, really hurts. I need to take off my boot."

Macy looked disgusted. Huffing, she clambered to her feet and walked over to the table. "Hey."

A rough hand pushed her away. "Not now, Macy."

"I need a knife."

Silence met Macy's request. A bottle clunked against the tabletop.

Macy thumbed in Andi's direction. "Her boot's gotta come off. Her foot's swellin' somethin' fierce."

Without a word, three sets of eyes turned and regarded Andi. She ducked her head. A crawly feeling crept up her spine. Everything inside screamed *run*. But she couldn't. *I wish I was invisible.*

A chair scraped against the floor. Andi's head snapped up.

Wild-haired Rudy rose. "Why, sure." He whipped a long, evil-looking knife from his belt. "I can take care o' that." He crossed the room and crouched beside Andi. "Your ankle feelin' poorly, rich girl?"

Andi glared at Rudy, stone-faced. Her stomach roiled.

Macy stood nearby, her face full of misgivings. "Rudy!" she squeaked. "Don't—"

"Shut up," Rudy snapped. Then he leered at Andi. "I bet under all that grime there's somethin' worth lookin' at. You might wash up real pretty." He set down his knife and reached out to rub her dusty cheek.

In a flash, Andi erupted. She snatched Rudy's hand and bit down hard. He reeled backward, roaring his pain and fury. "Don't touch me!" she yelled. Fear and rage jabbed her mind, blocking out the agony in her foot.

Rudy sucked on his bloodied hand. From the center of the room, Ty and Jase roared with laughter. Rudy lunged. "I'll do more than touch you, you little—"

"Don't try it." Faster than Andi could blink, Macy snatched Rudy's knife from the floor and pointed it at him. "I'll stick this in your gut if you don't mind your manners."

Rudy froze, eyes wide. Then he swore and backed up a step. "What's got into *you?*"

"Somethin' that shoulda a long time ago," Macy said. Her hands began to shake. So did her voice. "I ain't a baby no more, somebody you can boss around and thrash when you get the notion. And this girl? She ain't worth nothin' beat up or dead. If you can't figure that out then—"

"You made your point, Macy," Ty said quietly. No one was laughing now. "Rudy's just havin' some fun. He don't mean nothin' by it."

Andi disagreed. Rudy's eyes burned with more than annoyance at his sister for breaking up his fun. Macy had challenged him, a foolish and dangerous act. Andi was grateful to Macy, but she doubted the red-haired beast would forgive what his sister had done.

Rudy grunted and backed into his chair. "Gimme my knife."

"Not 'til I get the boot off." Putting words into action, Macy squatted next to Andi's foot and began to saw through the leather. "This is gonna hurt."

It did. By the time Andi's boot fell clear, she was clenching her fists and sobbing quietly. Her injury was a sorry sight. Purple and black mottling spread out from her swollen ankle and into the heel of her foot.

"Got yourself the dickens of a sprain," Ty said when he looked it over. He grinned. "Looks like I won't have to tie you up." He took the knife and returned to the table, where the brothers appeared to be making plans. Backs to the girls, they talked too softly to be overheard.

Andi wiped her wet face with her sleeve. Her foot still throbbed, but the pressure was off. "Thank you," she whispered. "And not just for getting my boot off."

Macy glanced nervously in her brothers' direction before replying softly, "Don't know what came over me. Always been too scared to stand up to 'em. But Rudy's a mean one. I couldn't let him hurt you." She gave Andi the ghost of a grin. "You *bit* him." She clapped a hand over her mouth to muffle her laughter.

A chair scraped, and Macy slammed back against the wall. When Ty caught her gaze, she griped, "How long do I hafta nursemaid this girl?"

Ty scowled at her and turned back to his planning.

Unlike Macy, Andi didn't find anything funny about the knife incident. Ty seemed to have a measure of control over his brothers, but that Rudy character was creepy, with a hair trigger. "Aren't you afraid he'll come after you?"

Macy shrugged. "Ty won't let him . . ." Her voice trailed off to a whispered, "I hope." She leaned her head back and closed her eyes.

Andi slumped against the rough boards, hurting and exhausted. No one had offered her a blanket, and nights in this secluded canyon were chilly. A breeze carrying the ever-present summer dust blew in through the cracked door and settled on her. She shivered. As tired as Andi felt, she couldn't sleep. Not with three dangerous men sitting there planning her fate. Coarse laughter and clinking bottles kept her wide awake.

"Bring me a sheet o' paper, Macy-gal, and a pencil." Ty's sharp command jerked Macy to her feet. She scurried to the fireplace and fumbled for her copybook on the narrow mantel. She ripped out a sheet and crossed to the table. Andi watched, wide-eyed.

"This for the ransom note?" Macy asked.

"Mebbe." With a swipe of his arm, Ty cleared a spot on the table. Whiskey bottles rolled off and crashed to the floor. "Depends on how much we can get. Might be easier to kill her and cut our losses."

Macy shuddered. "I get all jittery thinkin' about killin' somebody outright like that. Her family would pay good money for her, maybe a couple thousand dollars."

"You think they'd pay as much as *that*?" Rudy's voice sounded shrill with shock.

"Yeah." Macy nodded. "Y'all forgot I went to school with these do-gooders. I know 'em. The Carters love this girl. She's the *baby*, the pampered pet o' her family. They'll pay plenty to get her back."

Andi cringed. She had never thought of herself as spoiled or over-indulged. Dearly loved, yes. Pampered? No. Mother and Justin and especially Chad were always ready to put her in her place. But Macy's words were a wake-up call. *I will not get angry the next time Chad scolds me*, she promised herself.

If there *was* a next time.

Macy was still talking. "I could write y'all a fine note. With so much money we could forget about stealin' cattle an' horses and go to Oregon. Or Nevada. Get ourselves a spread and live like regular folks."

A long pause followed Macy's speech. Ty looked at his sister as if he didn't quite know what to make of her. "Maybe this tadpole's got a good plan," he admitted. "Now ain't ya glad I made her go to school?" He aimed his question at Rudy, who scowled at Macy.

Macy leaned over the table and smoothed out the paper. "What'd y'all want me to write?"

Ty tipped back in his chair. He crossed his arms and stared at the ceiling, pondering. "Let's see. How 'bout this?" He cleared his throat. "If you want your girl back, put two thousand dollars in saddle bags and leave it—"

"Hold on," Macy said. "I can't spell that fast." She scratched away for a minute then looked up.

"Leave it in the old claim shanty at Watts Spring," Ty finished.

Macy wrinkled her forehead. "Ain't ya gonna tell 'em where to find her?"

Ty exchanged cautious glances with Jase and Rudy before replying. "Oh, yeah. Sure. 'When we get the money, we'll tell you where to find the girl.'" His chair legs slammed down. "That's it. They don't need no more."

"Who's gonna deliver it?" Jase asked.

"I will," Macy offered. "I know where they live."

Jase snorted. "You and the rest of the valley."

Andi's heart plunged clear to her throbbing ankle. *Macy, you can't leave me here alone!*

"A scruffy stranger ridin' up to their ranch'll make 'em suspicious," Macy countered. "It's best if I—"

"No." Rudy whirled on his sister. He clamped a meaty hand around Macy's wrist and squeezed. She yelped. "You ain't goin'." He jerked his chin in Andi's direction. "You say she ain't your friend, but I got eyes. You two been actin' thick as thieves over there. *I'll* do it." He glanced at Ty, who nodded. "I'll ride up, pitch a rock through their fancy window, and keep goin'."

Macy narrowed her eyes. "You'll get caught."

Rudy give his sister an evil smirk. "That would be too bad for your . . . *friend.*" He shoved Macy away and stood up. "One more thing so the Carters know we mean business."

Andi shrank back in terror when the redheaded beast squatted beside her. With his left hand, he gripped the back of her neck. His other hand—the one Andi had bloodied—slid his knife from its sheath.

"Rudy!" Macy threw herself on his back and clawed at him. "What kinda stupid and spiteful—"

Ty ripped Macy away. "Stay outta this."

Slowly, as if savoring the moment, Rudy laid the knife's cold edge against Andi's throat. She sucked in a shallow breath and held it. Tears stung her eyes but she didn't blink. Her heart pounded in her ears. Deathly afraid, she no longer felt the throbbing of her ankle or any other pain. She closed her eyes and made no sound. Not even a whimper.

"That's right. Hold real still," Rudy ordered. "I got slippery fingers."

Andi's fear grew. She couldn't scream and she was too scared to pray. Dizziness engulfed her. Then suddenly a peace she couldn't explain settled over her. A Bible verse whispered in her head. *"Lo, I am with you . . ."* She felt warm all over and opened her eyes.

Rudy's monstrous head hung only inches from her face. His whiskey breath made her gag. "I ain't forgettin' what you done t' me," he whispered. "I intend to pay you back . . . but all in good time." He shifted his knife to a tendril of hair that had escaped Andi's braid. With one slice, her long, dark waves dangled from Rudy's hand.

He stood up. "This'll prove we got the girl."

Andi collapsed in a heap and wept.

Macy whirled on Ty. "That was mean. You coulda stopped him."

Ty cuffed her. "You're gettin' too big for your britches, girl." He clapped Rudy on the back. "Get goin'. You'll need to hide out near the spring and wait for the drop. Then get back here quick as you can."

Rudy nodded. "I'm on it." He stuffed the note and Andi's hair in his pocket, grabbed a lantern, and slammed through the door. A dreadful silence fell.

Andi swallowed. "W-when Rudy brings the money you'll let me go, right?"

Ty eyed her. "Sure, girlie. We'll leave ya right here." He opened a bottle of whiskey and took a swig.

Then he laughed.

CHAPTER 25

Who would have guessed? Macy turned out to be a friend "that sticketh closer than a brother."

"Andi."

Andi batted at the niggling voice that poked at her mind. *Go away. It's such a nice dream . . .*

"Andi!" A rough shake accompanied the voice this time, rousing Andi from a deep sleep. Her dream of romping with Shasta and Sunny shattered, replaced by shooting pain in her ankle and a throbbing headache. She moaned and sat up. Her tongue felt like cotton.

Macy clapped a hand over Andi's mouth. "Shhh. Not a peep. Not if you wanna save your skin." She shook all over. Her eyes were huge and dark with worry.

Andi's groggy mind spun. *Where am I?* It all came back in a flash. She was trapped in a drafty, filthy shack. The air reeked of stale whiskey. The lantern had gone out, but a pale dawn shone through the hut's one window. Sprawled out on bedrolls in the corners, two dark figures lay snoring.

Macy removed her hand. She flicked a wary glance at her slumbering brothers before turning back to Andi. "We gotta go."

Andi sucked in her breath. She wasn't going anywhere. Not with her ankle swollen enough to belong in a circus sideshow. *Like a human freak,* she thought with a shudder. Now that she was awake, the rest of her body felt beat up. Her scraped arm was stiff and sore; her shoulders ached.

"I hurt too much. Can't we wait 'til Rudy gets back? He'll bring the money and . . ." Her whispers died away at Macy's wagging head. "What's wrong?"

"It ain't gonna happen the way you think." Macy kept her voice low. "I heard Jase and Ty arguin' when they thought I was asleep. Soon as Rudy gets back with the money they're gonna get rid of you."

Sudden panic welled up inside Andi. She'd counted on being left behind. No one here knew she'd left clues to her whereabouts. The Walkers would take the money and clear out of the canyon. If they didn't tell her family where she was, her brothers would find her anyway. End of story.

Tears blurred her vision at this deadly twist. "But Ty said he'd leave—"

"Ty lies a lot," Macy cut in. "They don't wanna take any chances. Witnesses help sheriffs make wanted posters. They're not funnin', Andi. They mean it. I . . . I seen 'em do it before." A thumping noise spun Macy around. One brother turned over, muttered obscenities in his sleep, and resumed snoring. Macy clutched Andi's arm. "We gotta go *now*, before Rudy gets back."

"Go where?" Andi whispered.

"I know a spot near the back of the canyon. Lots of brush and scrubby trees. It's boggy, but if we keep hid, the boys might give up lookin' for us. Then I could go for help."

Andi's mouth dropped open. "Do you know what you're saying? That means—"

"Yeah. I'm stayin' behind." Macy took a deep, shuddering breath. "It was a different story when it was just the colts. But I can't let 'em kill you. I'll help you outta this fix, Andi, even if it means givin' up my brothers."

"You won't be alone," Andi promised. "You can stay with me and my family. You'll be more than welcome."

Macy knuckled her eyes. "Quit talkin' foolish." When she looked at Andi her eyes were puffy, but they blazed with resolve. "I don't care if you're hurtin'. You're gonna stand up and lean on me. Clamp your jaw shut when you feel like yellin'."

Andi nodded and let Macy pull her up from the floor. A cry raced through her throat but she swallowed it. She wrapped her right arm around Macy's shoulder and clenched her teeth.

"I ain't big," Macy whispered. "But I'm strong and wiry. You keep your good foot hoppin'—quiet-like—and I'll hold you up." She pulled open the back door.

Creak! Andi froze. Sweat broke out on her forehead. She listened. Macy's brothers slept on. When she didn't move, Macy hissed, "Let's go, for pity's sake."

Outdoors, the early morning rays bathed the canyon in a soft, warm light. Birds chirped. A dragonfly swooped. It felt so ordinary and welcoming that Andi couldn't believe she was running for her life through a hazardous canyon. *Not running,* she corrected. *Hobbling.* Every time she took a step, pain exploded where falling debris had bruised her good leg a few hours ago.

"We're headed yonder." Macy pointed to a massive boulder a hundred yards away. Behind it, leafy cottonwoods and aspens rose. The canyon narrowed and ended just beyond the rock. Sheer cliffs soared upward on all sides.

Andi and her human crutch stumbled past the corral. The two colts whinnied to be let out. When the girls hurried by without stopping, the horses neighed unhappily and galloped around the enclosure. "Hurry," Macy urged. "Their racket might wake the boys."

Halfway to the boulder, Andi lagged. Her head spun. *I can't go any farther.* For the first time in her life she was too tired to fight. She hurt too much to go on. She crumpled to the ground. Macy fell with her. "This is far enough," Andi managed between gasps.

Macy shot to her feet. "No, it ain't."

"I feel sick."

"Get up," Macy said frantically. "Get up or I'll drag ya." To prove her point, she latched onto Andi's arms and yanked.

One tug convinced Andi that her friend meant business. Being dragged along the rocky ground hurt twice as much as hobbling. She staggered up, squeezed her eyes shut, and let Macy carry her along.

Ten minutes later Andi and Macy huddled together beneath the overhanging branches of cottonwoods and young willows. The ground nearby was a bog; dark water oozed up between grassy hummocks.

"We must be close to the spring." Andi slapped her cheek when a mosquito landed. "I could sure do with something to drink."

"Pesky skeeters. Gonna eat us alive by the time we get outta here." Macy slapped her bare arms. "Rest first. We'll find the spring later. You look plumb wore out."

Andi nodded miserably. Thirst or no thirst, she could not go another step. She settled back in the marshy grass and willed her aches and pains to go away. At least the discomfort of needing the privy had been taken care of a few minutes before. "How long?" she asked.

Macy's eyebrows shot up. "Huh?"

"How long do you think we'll have to stay in this wretched canyon?"

"Depends on how it goes with the money." Macy shrugged. "The boys might look for ya. Then again, if they suspect somebody's after 'em, they'll take the money and light outta here quick." She looked wistfully in the direction of the shack.

Andi propped herself up against a rough willow trunk and followed Macy's gaze. *It must be awful for Macy to turn her back on her brothers. They're worthless, but those three are her family.* Andi pondered. Maybe her friend needn't lose them. It was time to tell Macy the truth. "You can go back," she said softly. "Maybe you can convince them to leave. You don't need to stay with me. I'll keep hidden. My brothers will find me."

"What? How?"

Andi bit her lip. It was best to spill it fast and get it over with. "They . . ." She swallowed and tried again. "My family knows where I am." *I hope.*

Macy's eyes grew round.

"I didn't tell them. Honest. But I did write everything down in my journal. I left it out where somebody would find it if I didn't show up back home." She sighed. "I'm sorry, Macy. I couldn't take off without leaving some kind of message. I'm sure someone's seen it by now." She bowed her head and waited for Macy to tear into her for breaking her promise.

Macy sat stock-still. When Andi looked up, she gave her a quick nod. "Good."

"But—"

"I ain't mad," Macy said. She started crying. "If I had a family like yours, I woulda done the same thing so they wouldn't worry none." She shook her head. "I'm sick of my brothers' fool notions. Last year they held up stagecoaches. I had to keep the horses outta sight. I was scared spitless the whole time, 'specially when a bullet whizzed past my ear." She sniffed. "I never had the grit to stand up to 'em before. Had no place to go even if I did. But I do now." Her voice turned firm. "I ain't leavin' you."

Andi didn't get the chance to answer. A loud string of swearing brought both girls up and alert. Macy's face reddened. "My brothers really know how to cuss."

"I th-think they figured out we're gone," Andi stammered. She couldn't run; she couldn't walk. If Ty or Jase saw her, it was all over.

Andi spent the next few minutes cowering in the bushes. She couldn't see Macy's brothers, but she heard them loud and clear. They screamed and yelled, threatening Macy with dire consequences if she didn't show her face in ten seconds.

"Just lay low," Macy advised. "They'll get tired of rantin' pretty soon." She scrunched up her face in thought. "I don't hear Rudy. He's the one to watch out for. Wonder why he ain't back yet. If he gets here soon, they might take off and leave us be."

"You really are burning your bridges, aren't you?" Andi said. "You won't be sorry. Justin can make everything all legal and—"

"*Hush!*" Macy ordered. She lifted her head above a clump of marsh grass. "Do you hear that?"

Andi listened. Above the Walker brothers' tirade, cattle were lowing close by. The colts were at it again in the distance, whinnying their discontent. They were probably hungry and thirsty. *Just like me*, Andi mused.

The voices grew silent. The cattle noises drew nearer. Crackling and snapping, three brown and white steers broke through the curtain of willows and splashed into the bog. Andi gasped. What dumb cows would willingly venture into a marsh?

There was only one explanation. Macy's brothers must be nearby, disrupting the cattle and searching every square inch of the canyon. Andi gulped and shrank back into the vegetation. She pricked up her ears to listen for the slightest sound. A branch broke. Through the thick brush, Andi spied an approaching figure. She closed her eyes and prayed, *Please, God, help us!*

Macy nudged her. Andi opened her eyes and glanced down. Her heart nearly slammed through her chest. A shiny Colt revolver lay across Macy's palm, dwarfing her hand. "Just in case," she whispered.

In case of *what*? Andi wanted to shriek.

"I snitched it after they fell asleep. Thought it might come in handy."

"You'd shoot your own brothers?" Andi choked back her horror.

"Shhh!" Macy looked scared but determined. "Only if I have to. I won't let 'em hurt you . . . or me."

Another branch snapped. Andi heard squishing, a splash, then cursing. "I know you're back there." Jase's voice cracked like a gunshot. "I ain't foolin' around, Macy. Get yer worthless, double-crossin' hide out here or I'll start shootin' anything that moves." He shot off two rounds to prove his point.

Andi and Macy exchanged hopeless looks. Macy raised the pistol and cocked it. The sound brought Jase tearing through the saplings. "That's far enough," Macy said.

Jase froze. His gun hung loosely at his side. "What's this, Macy? A knife for Rudy? A bullet for me?" He laughed, but it sounded forced. His eyes told Andi the story. He was afraid of this new Macy. He took a step back.

"If you lift that pistol, I'll shoot," Macy said.

"You won't shoot your own brother." He raised his gun.

Crack!

Jase howled and clutched his hand. His weapon plunked into the marsh.

"I've got no problem shooting you," a new voice growled. "Raise your hands and back away from the girls. If you so much as twitch I'll make the next shot count."

Jase scrambled to obey. He slipped, tripped, and landed in the bog with a loud *splash*. Chad yanked him up by his collar and handed him over to one of the other rescuers. Then he slipped his pistol into his holster and started forward.

Andi's heart leaped with joy. She grabbed Macy and squeezed her tight. "They came," she squealed. "They found us, just like I knew they would."

Macy uncocked her pistol and let it drop to the ground. Tears streaming, she returned Andi's hug. By the time Chad and Mitch fought their way through the underbrush, the girls were blubbering, locked in each other's arms. Andi couldn't stop crying, not even when Chad gently peeled her hands away from Macy and gathered her up in his arms.

"My, my, don't we look fetching this morning?" he teased. Then he held her close, and his voice turned comforting. "Shhh. It's all over. We caught the other one near the corral and nabbed the note-carrier hours ago." He let out a deep sigh. "Thank God we got here in time."

Mitch helped Macy from the thicket. Together they headed across the canyon floor for home and safety.

Thank God, indeed! Andi thought. *And thank You, God, for a friend like Macy.*

CHAPTER 26

I hope Macy wants to stay on the ranch. She seems happy, but I often catch a restless, faraway look in her eyes. The Circle C must not feel like home to her yet. I wonder what it will take to make her feel like she belongs.

It was a Fourth of July Andi would never forget. Her brothers whisked her home in the early morning hours and Dr. Weaver carefully tended her sprained ankle. He treated her other scrapes and bruises with a *tsk-tsk* and said it was high time she stopped behaving like such a rough-and-tumble tomboy. Mother made sure Andi kept still. It felt heavenly to lie on the settee on soft cushions, floating in and out of blessed sleep, and to have her meals served.

The first couple days at home flew by. From the splintering of the window during the middle of the night to the surprise of finding Taffy and the foals wandering around the yard, Chad and Mitch filled Andi's ears with a running account of the events leading up to the rescue.

"You never saw anybody act more shook up than that Rudy fellow when he was caught so fast. The ranch has been pretty lively at night the past month. He didn't stand a chance." Mitch laughed and slapped his knee. "He nearly burst a blood vessel when we told him we already knew where you were and what he and his brothers were up to out at Rock Canyon."

"We finally had to gag him to shut him up." Chad chuckled. "Never did tell him how we knew." He tweaked Andi's hair. "That journal came in handy, little sister." His next words made her stomach squeeze. "I don't know what we'd have done without it."

Andi knew. She would either be abandoned or dead.

All too quickly, though, Andi tired of her brothers' stories. She itched to get off the couch. Macy spent her days romping with Andi's colts while Andi lay around fretting. Mitch dropped a stack of dime novels on the table. Melinda brought a sewing basket full of quilt patches. The dime novels won.

Two weeks later, Andi looked up from reading *Buckskin Sam, the Scalp Taker* and caught Macy standing uncertainly in the parlor doorway. She looked lost and uncertain. *I reckon I'd look and feel the same way if my brothers had been arrested and dragged off to jail.* Chad and Mitch had been careful to recount their tales out of Macy's earshot, but she certainly knew the facts.

"Come in, Macy." Andi waved from the settee. Her bandaged ankle lay propped up on a pile of fluffy pillows. "Tell me about the colts. You're making them behave, right? Especially Sunny?" Andi wouldn't be training her colts anytime soon. Doctor Weaver had given an ultimatum: stay put for at least three weeks, or else. "Worst sprain I've ever treated," he'd scolded.

Macy entered the parlor with a sudden smile. Eagerness replaced her lonely, hungry expression. "The colts are fine." She settled herself on a slice of sofa next to Andi. "None the worse for their adventure. Sunny's been eatin' outta my hand every day."

"I'm glad," Andi said. "Chad says they found the last of the missing colts yesterday. And Apache made it back in one piece too." She frowned. "I sure hate getting news secondhand."

"I can be your eyes and ears for a spell," Macy said. "I heard one o' your hands yellin' in Spanish the other day." She giggled. "He had to nursemaid the left-behind steers through the gap one at a time. Took him hours and hours. Guess the critters didn't wanna leave."

Andi laughed. She'd already heard the tale when Rosa brought Andi her lunch tray. They'd both howled.

Macy lowered her voice. "Did you hear that your brother and his intended put off their weddin' 'til you're up and about?"

Andi nodded. "Lucy told me yesterday. They don't want to carry me all the way to San Francisco." She reached out and clasped Macy's hand. "Oh, Macy! The reception's going to be at the Palace Hotel. Wait 'til you see it. The *Palace!*" Andi didn't care for San Francisco, but she did enjoy staying at the most luxurious hotel on the West Coast.

Macy lost her smile. "Listen, Andi. Your family's been good to me. I ain't never lived so high off the hog. Plenty to eat, new clothes, a bubble bath every day. I like bein' with Sunny too. And your ma acts like she really cares for me. Your sister's sweet, and your brothers . . ." She talked faster. "They're just what brothers should be—bossin' and teasin' most days, but carin' for ya when it counts." She twisted the folds of her skirt. "But . . ."

"But what?" Andi asked, stunned. "Don't you want to stay? I thought Justin was going to take care of it all legal-like."

Macy squirmed. "You make it sound right temptin'. But I talked to your brother. I got kinfolk, remember? Aunt Hester, well . . . I reckon I'm hankerin' to see what's become of her." She sighed. "It's been five years. Most likely she don't want nothin' to do with a ragamuffin like me."

Andi's heart dropped. Now that Rosa had "grown up," Andi hoped Macy would step in and share her adventures. *I won't let her see how disappointed I am.* "If your aunt is still alive, Justin can find her," she said, forcing a smile.

"Mebbe. Ain't no way to get there though."

"Would you like to go back to Arkansas, Macy?" Elizabeth Carter stood in the parlor doorway. Next to her, Melinda carried a silver tray with a tea service and a plate of sugar cookies.

Andi's mouth watered.

"I reckon so, ma'am," Macy said shyly. "Aunt Hester was good to me."

"What do you say we have a little tea party and discuss the possibility," Elizabeth suggested. Melinda set the tray down on a low table and began to pour the hot tea into cups.

"I think I'll join you if I can pass on the tea," a new voice called from the doorway.

"Sure, Justin." Andi motioned him into the room. "We're always looking to include a gentleman at our tea parties."

"Why, thank you." Justin entered and took a seat next to the ladies. "How are you this afternoon, my darling crippled sister?"

"Tired of sitting around," Andi answered. "What's in your hand?"

"You'll find out soon enough," Justin replied. He helped himself to a cookie.

Elizabeth sipped her tea and smiled at Macy. "We enjoy having you as part of our family, but we certainly understand if you'd like to be with your relatives."

Andi nodded but didn't say anything.

"What is on your heart, Macy?" Elizabeth probed gently. "What would you like to do most?"

Macy dropped her gaze to her lap. "I'd like to settle down with my kin if they'll have me. Blood's important. That's why Ty yanked me along with him in the first place. That notion stuck with me." She raised her head. "I don't mean t' be ungrateful or nothin'," she added quickly.

"We understand," Elizabeth assured her.

Macy let out a breath. "Good. I think I'd like to get me some more learnin' too. T'wasn't half-bad, lookin' back on the last few weeks of school."

"Yep," Andi agreed. "Once you start to learn things, you want to learn more."

Justin laughed. "Is that why it's so hard to get you out of the buggy to start a new term of school, young lady?"

Andi opened her mouth, flushed hotly, and closed her mouth. Then she did the only wise thing. She laughed with the others.

"Macy," Justin said, "I don't believe there will be any problem filling your requests." He lifted the envelope he was holding. "I received a telegram today from Fayetteville."

"Fayetteville, *Arkansas*?" Macy gasped and leaped to her feet. "Why, that's where Aunt Hester lived when I was little. She still lives there? You found her?"

Justin grinned. "Yes, Macy, to both questions."

Macy bit her lip. "Did you tell her about Ty and the others?"

"I did."

Macy stared at the envelope in Justin's hand. Her eyes turned worried when he held it out to her.

"Take it, Macy," Andi said. "See what it says."

"What if . . ." Macy's hand shook when she took the envelope. "What if Aunt Hester don't want an outlaw like me?"

Justin smiled. "You're not an outlaw, Macy. Open it."

With a heavy sigh, Macy tore open the envelope and unfolded the slip of paper. She scanned the message and frowned. "I can't read all them big words." She held it out to Andi. "Will you read it to me?"

Andi snatched the sheet of paper and read:

JUSTIN CARTER
FRESNO CALIFORNIA
MAKE IMMEDIATE ARRANGEMENTS FOR MY NIECE
MARCELLA TO RETURN TO ARKANSAS. HAVE MISSED
HER TERRIBLY. LOOK FORWARD TO SEEING HER SOON.
SENDING HER MY LOVE.
HESTER WALKER TRENT
FAYETTEVILLE ARKANSAS

"This is wonderful news," Andi said. She handed the telegram back to her friend. "I'll miss you, but I do understand the difference between staying with friends and staying with family."

Macy carefully replaced the telegram in the envelope and stuffed it in her skirt pocket. "Aunt Hester wants me back. She misses me." Her face was all smiles. "Thank you, Mr. Carter."

"My pleasure, Miss Walker. And I do mean that." He picked up Macy's hand and squeezed it. "Nothing we do for you can ever repay your part in saving Andi's life."

Macy looked embarrassed. She cleared her throat and said, "Well, I reckon I'd best get to packin'. I'm itchy to see the home folks. When do y'all think I can leave?"

"The end of the week," Justin assured her. He winked at Andi.

Andi nodded. She knew what Justin was waiting to hear. She'd already given Sunny to Macy in her heart. Andi had hoped she and her friend would ride the twins all over the ranch someday. That wouldn't happen now. Macy would ride Sunny in the Ozarks of Arkansas. "Yes," she said. "I think the end of the week should give Chad enough time to get Sunny ready."

"Ready for what?" Macy wrinkled her forehead.

"For his trip."

"Where's he goin'?" Macy demanded. "You ain't sold him without tellin' me, have you?" Fire burned in her pale-blue eyes. She clenched her fists.

Andi laughed at how quickly Macy could be stirred up. "He's going back East, Macy. With you."

Macy caught her breath. "You're funnin' me!" She looked helplessly around the room.

"I'm not kidding you," Andi said quietly. "I'm giving Sunny to you for your very own."

"B-but why?"

"Because you love him. And because of Sunny and Shasta, you decided to help me. If it weren't for you, my colts would be long gone and so would you and your brothers." Andi looked up into Macy's flushed face. "You went against your brothers and lost your family to rescue me and help me get my colts back. I want you to have Sunny. Please don't say no."

Macy licked her lips. "Can I ride with him in the livestock car so's he won't be scared?"

"We'll see," Justin said. "And I'll make sure you have plenty of money for the trip and for Sunny's care."

Macy's eyes shone with delight at owning the cream-colored colt. "My very own," she whispered. Then she turned to Andi. "Every time I ride Sunny I'll remember how you didn't never give up on me."

A lump lodged in Andi's throat. What if Mr. Foster had given in to her selfish whim and assigned her a new seat? The colts would be gone forever. Macy would still be an orphan outlaw. Shivers raced up Andi's neck when she realized how close she'd come to making the wrong decision about befriending the roughneck girl.

She swallowed the lump and smiled at Macy. "That's fine, Macy. Just fine."

Everything *was* fine.